I0670939

THE ASCENT OF THE SOUL

AMORY H. BRADFORD, D.D.

1st WORLD
LIBRARY
Literary Society

The Ascent of the Soul

Amory H. Bradford

© 1st World Library – Literary Society, 2005
PO Box 2211
Fairfield, IA 52556
www.1stworldlibrary.org
First Edition

LCCN: 2006902681

Softcover ISBN: 1-4218-1815-9
Hardcover ISBN: 1-4218-1715-2
eBook ISBN: 1-4218-1915-5

Purchase *"The Ascent of the Soul"*
as a traditional bound book at:
www.1stWorldLibrary.org/purchase.asp?ISBN=1-4218-1815-9

1st World Library Literary Society is a nonprofit
organization dedicated to promoting literacy by:

- Creating a free internet library accessible from any
  computer worldwide.
- Hosting writing competitions and offering book
  publishing scholarships.

**Readers interested in supporting literacy
through sponsorship, donations or
membership please contact:
literacy@1stworldlibrary.org
Check us out at: www.1stworldlibrary.ORG
and start downloading free ebooks today.**

The Ascent of the Soul
contributed by Tim, Ed & Rodney
in support of
1st World Library Literary Society

To The Memory of My Father

That each, who seems a separate whole,
Should move his rounds, and fusing all
The skirts of self again, should fall
Remerging in the general Soul,

Is faith as vague as all unsweet:
Eternal form shall still divide
The eternal soul from all beside;
And I shall know him when we meet.

In Memoriam.

INTRODUCTION

The purpose of the following chapters will be evident to all who may care to peruse them. I have endeavored simply to read the soul of man with something of the care that one reads a book containing a message which he believes to be of importance.

While one class of scientists are seeking to explore the physical universe, another class, with equal care, are studying the human spirit, and, already, startling discoveries have been made. My work is in no sense new in kind, but it is such as one whose whole time is devoted to dealing with the inner life would naturally give to such a subject. It hardly needs to be added that my method is practical rather than speculative. I am more interested in helping the ascent of the soul than in accounting for its origin. In carrying out my plan I have considered the following subjects: The nature and genesis of the soul, its awakening to a consciousness of responsibility, the steps which it first takes on its upward pathway, the experience of moral failure, its second awakening, which is to an appreciation that the universe is on its side, the part of Christ in promoting its awakening, the sense of spiritual companionship by which it is ever attended, the discipline of struggle, and the nurture and culture best fitted to promote its growth. I have also sought to read some of the prophecies of the soul, and have found them all pointing toward a continuance of its being beyond the event called death, and toward the fullness of Christ as the goal of humanity. I have found a place for prayers for the departed even among Protestants of the strictest sects.

A study of the soul, like a study of history, inspires optimism. It is hard to believe that it could have been intended first for perfection and then for extinction. It is equally difficult to believe that any soul will, in the end, be "cast as rubbish to the void."

In these studies I have tried ever to be mindful of my own limitations, and not to forget that a fraction of humanity can never hope to comprehend the fullness of truth. Of that side of the spiritual sphere which has been turned toward me, and of that alone, have I presumed to write. All that I claim for this book is that it is the contribution of one, anxious to know what is true, toward a better understanding of a subject which is daily receiving wider recognition and more thorough consideration.

AMORY H. BRADFORD.

MONTCLAIR, NEW JERSEY,
August 30, 1902.

CONTENTS

THE SOUL

It is no spirit who from heaven hath flown
And is descending on his embassy;
Nor traveler gone from earth the heaven t'espy!
'Tis Hesperus - there he stands with glittering crown,
First admonition that the sun is down, -
For yet it is broad daylight! - clouds pass by;
A few are near him still - and now the sky,
He hath it to himself - 'tis all his own.
O most ambitious star! an inquest wrought
Within me when I recognized thy light;
A moment I was startled at the sight;
And, while I gazed, there came to me a thought
That even I beyond my natural race
Might step as thou dost now: - might one day trace
Some ground not mine; and, strong her strength above,
My soul, an apparition in the place,
Tread there, with steps that no one shall reprove!

- Wordsworth

I

THE SOUL

Subjects which a few years ago were regarded as the exclusive property of cultured thinkers, are now common themes of thought and conversation. Psychology has been popularized. Materialistic doctrines are at a discount even in this age of physical science.

It is difficult to explain the somewhat sudden appearance of intense interest in questions which have to do with the life of the spirit; but, whatever the theory of its genesis, there is no doubt of its presence. This, therefore, is a favorable time for a somewhat extended study of the stages through which we pass in our spiritual growth. I shall endeavor to use the inductive method in this inquiry, and trust that I am not presumptuous in giving to these essays the title,

THE ASCENT OF THE SOUL.

The phrases, "The Ascent of Man" and "The Descent of Man" are familiar to all readers of the literature of modern science. One of the most eminent of American writers on science and philosophy too soon taken from his work, if any act of Providence is ever too soon, has made a clear distinction between evolution as applied to the body and as applied to the spirit. In lucid and luminous pages he has taught us that evolution, as a physical process, having culminated in man can go no further along those lines; that henceforward "the Cosmic force" will be expended in the perfection of the spirit, and that that process will require eternity to complete.

More perspicuously than any other author, John Fiske has introduced to modern English thought the conception of the ascent of the soul, considered in its relation to the individual and to the race.

This subject naturally divides itself into two departments, viz. - the ascent of each individual soul and, then, the far-off perfecting of humanity. I shall make suggestions along both lines of inquiry. I do not know of any writer who has, in a compact form, presented the results of such studies, although there have been illustrations, especially in literature, which indicate that many thinkers have had in mind the attempt to trace and describe the progress of the soul from its bondage to animalism toward its perfection and glory in the freedom of the spirit.

Goethe, in "Faust," has made an effort to follow the process by which a weak woman and a weaker man, ignorant of the forces struggling within them and susceptible to malign influences from without, through terrible mistakes and bitter failure, at length reach the heights of character.

The Trilogy of Dante is a study of the soul in its slow and painful passage from hell, through purgatory, to heaven. Perhaps, however, the noblest and truest effort in this direction to be found in the world's literature is "The Pilgrim's Progress," in which a man of glorious genius and vision, but without academic culture, reflecting too much the crude and materialistic theology of his time and condition, follows the progress of a soul in its movement from the City of Destruction to the City Celestial. The City of Destruction is the state of animalism and selfishness from which the race has slowly emerged; and the City Celestial is not only the Christian's heaven, but also the state of those who, having escaped from earthliness, having conquered animalism and risen into the freedom of the spirit, breathe the air and enjoy the companionship of the sons of God.

It is my purpose in a different way to attempt to trace some of the steps of what may be called the evolution of the spirit, or, in the light of modern knowledge, the growth of the soul as it moves upward. At the outset I must make it plain that I am speaking of evolution since the time when man as a spirit appeared. Given the spiritual being, what are the stages through which he will pass on his way to the goal toward which he is surely pressing?

Just here we should ask, What do we mean by the soul? The word is used in its popular sense, as synonymous with spirit or personality. Man has a dual nature; one part of his being is of the dust and to the dust it returns; the other part is a mystery; it is known only by what it does. Man thinks, loves, chooses, and is conscious of himself as thinking, loving, choosing. The unity of this being who thinks, loves, chooses in a single self-consciousness constitutes him a spirit, or personality; and that is what the word soul signifies in its popular usage. There is another technical definition which may be true or false but which is of no importance in our study.

The problem of life is the right adjustment of spirit and body, so that the former shall never be the servant but always the master of the latter.

We are on this earth, in the midst of darkness, with nothing absolutely sure except that in a little while we must die. We are two-fold beings in which there is war almost from the cradle to the grave, and that war is caused by the effort of the body to rule the soul and of the soul to conquer the body.

At the gates of this mystery we continually do cry, and little light comes from any quarter; indeed, it may be said no light except that of the Christian revelation, and the, as yet, not very pronounced prophecies of evolution.

One of the questions, which in all ages has been most

persistently asked, concerns the origin of the soul. Perhaps, in reality, that is no more mysterious than the genesis of the body; but the body is material and we live in a world of matter, and it is comparatively easy to see that our bodies are from the earth which they inhabit. Our souls, however, are invisible, immaterial, ethereal. There is no evident kinship between a thought and a stone, between love and the soil which produces vegetables, between a heroic choice and the stuff of the earth, between spirit and matter. Well, then, whence does the soul come?

It will be interesting at least to recall a few of the many answers which have been given to this inquiry.

One theory of the genesis of the soul is called Emanation. That means that in the universe there is really but one source of spiritual being, one Infinite Spirit, and that all other spiritual beings have proceeded from Him as the rays of light are flashed from the sun; and that, in time, all will return to Him again and be absorbed in the being from which they have come. Thus all spirits are supposed to have proceeded from one source - God. As all natural life in the end is but a manifestation of solar energy, so all human beings are supposed to be only bits of God, for a time imprisoned in bodies, and some time to return to the Deity and be absorbed in Him, or in it.

Another answer to the question as to the soul's origin is that of Preexistence. This may be called the Oriental theory, for almost the whole Orient holds this view. The substance of the teaching is suggested by Wordsworth, in his "Ode to Immortality," in the following lines:

"Our birth is but a sleep and a forgetting;
The soul that rises with us, our life's star,
Hath had elsewhere its setting,
And cometh from afar."

Many Occidentals have believed in preexistence. One of the

most intelligent persons whom I have ever known once affirmed that she had had thoughts which she was sure were memories of events which had occurred in a previous life. This answer only pushes the question one stage further back, and leaves us still inquiring, Where do the souls of men originally come from?

Another answer to our question affirms that every individual soul is created by God whenever a body is in readiness to receive it - that when a body is born a soul is made to order for it. An old poet wrote as follows:

"Then God smites His hands together
And strikes out a soul as a spark,
Into the organized glory of things,
From the deeps of the dark."[1]

[Footnote 1: W.R. Alger, "History of the Doctrine of a Future Life," page 10.]

The Greek myth of Prometheus is an illustration of this teaching, for "Prometheus is said to have made a human image from the dust of the ground, and then, by fire stolen from heaven, to have animated it with a living soul."[2]

[Footnote 2: W.R. Alger, "History of the Doctrine of a Future Life," page 10.]

Another answer teaches that all human souls have been derived by heredity from that of Adam. This is a speculation found in medieval theology, and in the Koran.

A fanciful theory suggests that all souls have been in existence since the universe was formed; that they are floating in space like rays of light; and that when a body comes into being a soul is drawn into it with its first breath, or first nourishment. This is pure imagination, but intelligent and earnest men have believed it to be the true solution of the problem.

One other answer to this question of origin teaches that souls are propagated in the same way and at the same time as bodies; that when a human being appears he is body and spirit; that both are born together, both grow together; and then, some add, both die together, while others believe that the spirit enters at death on a larger and freer stage of existence.

I have recalled these speculations concerning the soul in order to show that in all ages this question has been eagerly put and reverently pressed. How could it have been otherwise? And what more convincing evidence of the spiritual nature of man could be desired than that he asks such questions? Would a figure of clay ask whether it were the abode of a higher order of being? Dust asks no questions concerning personality; but intelligence can never be satisfied until it knows the causes of things.

What is the teaching of the New Testament concerning this subject? The attitude of Jesus toward all the great problems was the practical one. He attempted to shed no light on causes, but ever endeavored to show how to make the best of things as they are. Whence came the soul? we may ask of Him, but He will tell us that a far more important inquiry is, How may the soul be delivered from imperfection, suffering, and sin, and saved to its noblest uses and loftiest possibilities?

The reality of spirit is everywhere assumed in the teaching of Jesus, but nowhere does there appear any effort to throw light on the mystery of its genesis.

The distinction between spirit and body is indicated by the Transfiguration, the Resurrection, the narratives of the continued existence of Jesus after His Crucifixion, by many references to the heavenly life, and by the appeals and invitations of the Gospel which are all addressed to intelligence and will. The presence of Jesus in history is an assertion of the spiritual nature of man. Various philosophers have tried to satisfy the desire for light on the question of the origin of personality; but Jesus has told us how, being here, we may break our prison-houses and rise into the full freedom and glory of the children of God. While inquirers have been seeking light, Jesus has brought to them salvation; while they have fruitlessly asked whence they came, Jesus has told them whither they are going.

The real problem of human life is not one which has to do with our birth, but with our destiny. We know that we think, choose, love; we know that we are self-conscious; we feel that we have kinship with something higher than the ground on which we walk. The stars attract us because they are above and have motion, but the earth we tread upon has few fascinations.

Jesus has responded to the essential questions: For what have we been created? What is our true home? What is the goal of personality? By what path does man move from the bondage of his will, and the limitation of his animalism toward the glorious liberty of the children of God, and toward the fullness of his possible being?

We are thus brought face to face with other questions of deep importance What part do weakness, limitation, suffering, sorrow, and even sin, play in the development of souls? Is it necessary that any should fall in order that they may rise? Did John Bunyan truly picture the ascent of the soul? Does its path, of necessity, lead through the Slough of Despond, through Vanity Fair, by Castle Dangerous, and into the realm of Giant Despair?

Must one pass through hell and purgatory before he may enjoy the "beatific vision?" Are temptation, sin, sorrow, and even death, angels of God sent forth to minister to the perfection of man? or are they fiends which, in some foul way, have invaded the otherwise fair regions in which we dwell?

These are some of the questions to which we are to seek answers in the pages which are to follow. I am persuaded that, as the result of our studies, we shall find that the same beneficent hand which led the "Cosmic process" for unnumbered ages, until the appearance of man, is leading it still, that far more wonderful disclosures are waiting for the children of men as they shall be prepared to receive them, and that the glory of the "Spiritual Universe," as it approaches its consummation, when compared with the finest growths of character yet seen, will transcend them as the ordered creation, with its countless stars, transcends the primeval chaos.

In the meantime it is well to remember a few very simple and self-evident facts. One of these is that human souls must vary, at least as much as the bodies in which they dwell. Individuality has to do with spirits. We think, love, and choose in ways that differ quite as much as our bodily appearance. There is no uniformity in the spiritual sphere; - this we know from its manifestations in conduct and history. One man is heroic and another tender, one a reformer and another a recluse, one conservative and another radical. The same Bible has passages as widely contrasted as the twenty-third and the fifty-eighth Psalms, and characters as unlike as Jacob and Jesus. Indeed, may it not be assumed that physical differences are but expressions of still more clearly marked differences in spirits? If this is true it will follow that, as we move toward the goal of our being, while all will be under the same good care, we will move along different, though converging, paths. There are many roads to the "Celestial City" and, possibly, some of them do not lead through the Slough of Despond, or go very near to the realms of Giant Despair.

I cannot leave this part of my subject without dwelling for a moment upon two thoughts which to me seem to be full of significance.

This wonderfully complex nature of ours, - this power of thinking, choosing, loving, these mysterious inner depths out of which come strange suggestions, and within which, all the time, processes are carried on which may rise into consciousness and startle with their beauty or shame with their ugliness - does no suggestion come from it concerning its origin and destiny? Until they pass mid-life few men realize the terrible significance of the command of the oracle at Delphi, "Know Thyself." Who is not surprised every day at what he finds within himself? It sometimes seems as if two beings dwelt in every body, one in the region of consciousness, and one down below consciousness steadily forging the material which, sooner or later, must be forced up for the conscious man to think about.

In proportion as we know ourselves more accurately it becomes increasingly evident that as spirits we are allied to the great Spirit. Few who earnestly think can believe that their power of thought could have grown out of the earth; few when they love can believe that there is no fountain of love, unlimited and free; and few, when they choose one course and refuse another, would be willing to affirm that they are without the power of choice, and have no destiny but the grave. In other words, is not the fact that we are spirits all the proof that we need to have of the Father of Spirits? Is not a single ray of light all the evidence which any one needs of the reality of the sun? Is not the presence of one spiritual being a demonstration of a greater Spirit somewhere? Every soul indicates that, whatever the process by which it has reached its present development, it came originally from God. "In the beginning God" is a phrase which applies to the spiritual as well as to the material universe.

The soul is not only a witness concerning its own origin, but it is also a prophecy concerning its destiny. The more thoroughly it is studied the more convincing becomes the evidence that it must some time reach its perfected state. The perfection of intelligence, love, and will require endless growth. The great words of Pascal can hardly be recalled too frequently:

"Man is but a reed, the weakest in nature, but he is a thinking reed. It is not necessary that the entire universe arm itself to crush him. A breath of air, a drop of water suffices to kill him. But were the universe to crush him, man would still be more noble than that which kills him, because he knows that he dies; and the universe knows nothing of the advantage it has over him."

We can as yet hardly begin to comprehend that for which we were created; - now we see through a glass darkly. A caterpillar on the earth cannot appreciate a butterfly in the air. Jesus was the typical man, as well as the revelation of God. St. Paul has set our thoughts moving toward the "fullness of Christ" as the final goal of humanity. We may not, for many milleniums, know all that is contained in that phrase "the fullness of Christ;" but no one ever attentively listened to the voices which speak in his own soul, no one has even asked himself the meaning of the fact that nothing earthly ever completely satisfies, no one ever saw another in the ripeness of splendid powers growing more intelligent, loving, and spiritually beautiful, without feeling that if death were really the end no being is so much to be pitied as man, and no fate so much to be coveted as a short life in which the mockery may go on.

Our souls themselves assure us that they have come from a fountain of spiritual being - that is, from God; and they are also prophecies of a perfection which has never yet been realized on the earth and which will require eternity to complete. But all are not conscious of themselves as spiritual beings and children of eternity, and many come slowly to that consciousness. Our next inquiry, therefore, will concern the Soul's Awakening.

THE AWAKENING OF THE SOUL

There's a palace in Florence, the world knows well,
And a statue watches it from the square,
And this story of both do our townsmen tell.

Ages ago, a lady there,
At the farthest window facing the East
Asked, Who rides by with the royal air?

*   *   *   *   *

That selfsame instant, underneath,
The Duke rode past in his idle way
Empty and fine like a swordless sheath.

*   *   *   *   *

He looked at her, as a lover can;
She looked at him as one who awakes:
The past was a sleep, and her life began.

- The Statue and the Bust. Browning

II

THE AWAKENING OF THE SOUL

The process of physical awakening is not always sudden or swift. The passage from sleep to consciousness is sometimes slow and difficult. The soul's realization of itself is often equally long delayed. The effect of eloquence on an audience has often been observed when one by one the dormant souls wake up and begin to look out of their windows, the eyes, at the speaker who is addressing them. In something the same way the souls of men come to a consciousness of their powers and, with clearness, begin to look out on their possibilities and their destiny.

The prodigal son in the parable of Jesus lived his earlier years without an appreciation either of his powers or possibilities. When he came to himself this appreciation flashed upon his will and he turned toward his father.

Two chapters of this book will have to do with thoughts suggested by this "pearl of parables," viz., the Soul's Awakening and its Re-awakening. Before this young man decided to return to his father he knew himself as an intelligent and as a responsible being; the power of choice was not given him then for the first time. Long ere this he had decided how he would use his wealth. He knew the difference between right and wrong. He was intellectually and morally awake before he saw things in their true relations. "The wine of the senses" intoxicated him; the delights of the flesh seemed the only pleasures to be desired. At first he did not discover the essential excellence of virtue or the sure results of vice. Later, when he saw things in a clearer light, their proper proportions and relations appeared, and he came to himself and made the wise choice.

In this chapter we are to study the process of the soul's awakening to a consciousness of its powers, and in a subsequent chapter that re-awakening which is so radical as to merit the name it has usually received, viz., the new birth.

There is a time when the soul first realizes itself as a personality with definite responsibilities and relations. This experience comes to some earlier, and to some with greater vividness, than to others. So long as we are blind to our powers, responsibilities, relations, we can hardly be said to be spiritually awake. He only is awake who knows himself as a personality; who has heard the voice of duty; who, to some extent, appreciates the fact that he is dependent on a higher personality or power; and who recognizes that he is surrounded by other personalities who also have their rights, responsibilities, and relations. I think, I choose, I love, I know that I am dependent upon a Being higher than myself. I see that I am related to other personalities with rights as sacred as my own, and, therefore, that I must choose, think, love so as to be acceptable to the One to whom I am responsible, and harmonious with those by whom I am surrounded.

The soul's awakening is primarily a recognition and an appreciation of its responsibility. It may think, choose, love, without realizing responsibility, and, therefore, live as if it were the only being in the universe; but the moment it recognizes responsibility it also discerns a higher Person, and other persons, since responsibility to no one, and for nothing, is inconceivable.

The soul's awakening, therefore, carries with it the idea of obligation, and that includes the recognition of God, of duty, of right and wrong, in short, of a moral ideal. I do not mean to

Amory H. Bradford

insist that every one appreciates all that is implied in consciousness of responsibility. There are degrees of alertness, and some men are wide awake and others half asleep.

However it may have come to its self-realization, that is a solemn and sublime moment when a human soul understands, ever so dimly, that it is facing in the unseen Being one on whom it knows itself to be dependent; and when it discerns the hitherto invisible lines which bind it to other personalities, in all space and time. At that moment life really begins. Henceforward, by various ways, over undreamed-of obstacles, assisted by invisible hands, hindered by unseen forces, in spite of foes within and enemies without, the course of that soul must ever be toward its true home and goal, in the bosom of God.

The difficulties in the way of such a faith for the thoughtful and sensitive are many and serious. Not all blossoms come to fruitage; not all human beings are fit to live; processes of degeneration seem to be at work in nature, in society, and in the individual life.

Apparently true and time-honored interpretations of Scripture are quoted against the faith that in some way, and by some kind of discipline, the souls of men will forever approach God; while the belief of the church, so far as it has found expression in the creeds is urged in opposition. But when I see how timidly the creeds of the church have been held by many in all ages, how large a number of the most spiritual and morally earnest have questioned them at this point, and how often they have been rejected in whole, or in part, by those who have dared to trust their hearts; when I remember that the Scripture quoted as opposing is susceptible of another interpretation, when I remember that blossoms are not men, and, most of all when I see the God-like possibilities in every human being, I cannot resist the conviction that every soul of man is from God, and that, sometime and somehow, it may be by the hard path of retribution, possibly through great agonies and by means of austere chastisements and severe discipline as well as by loving entreaty, after suffering shall have accomplished all its ministries it will reach a blissful goal and the "beatific vision."

The awakening of the soul is its entrance upon an appreciation of its powers, relations, possibilities, and responsibilities.

What awakens the soul? The answer to that question is hidden. The wind bloweth where it listeth. Elemental processes and forces are all silent and viewless. The stillness of the sunrise is like that of the deeps of the sea. No eye ever traced the birth of life, and no sound ever attended the awakening of the soul; and yet this subject is not altogether mysterious. A few rays of light have fallen upon it. I venture suggestions which may help a little toward a rational answer to this question.

The soul awakens because it grows, and its growth is sure. Everything that is alive must grow; only death is stationary. It is as natural for us sometime to know ourselves as having relations both to the seen and the unseen as for our bodies to increase in stature. The Confession of Augustine[3] is true of all, "Thou madest us for Thyself, and our heart is restless until it repose in Thee."

[Footnote 3: Confessions. Book I, 1.]

The soul turns toward God as naturally as children turn toward their parents. I know no other way of explaining the fact that in all ages the majority of the people have had faith in some kind of a deity; and that, widely as they differ as to what is right, all feel that they should follow their convictions of duty. The various ethnic religions, however repulsive, cruel, and vile some of their teachings may be, all indicate a realization of dependence, and all, in some way, bear witness to man's longing for God. Augustine was right - "The heart is restless until it repose in Thee."

The healthful soul will always move along the pathway of growth. The next stage in its evolution after its birth is its awakening. Its progress may be hindered, but it cannot be prevented, and it may be hastened.

The means by which a soul comes to its self-realization has been a favorite study with poets, dramatists, and novelists. Marguerite, in "Faust," was a simple, sweet, sensuous, traditionally religious girl until she was rudely startled by the knowledge that she was a great sinner; that moment the scales began to fall from her eyes. In her, Goethe has shown how one class of persons, and that a large class, come to self-realization.

Victor Hugo, in a passage of almost unparalleled pathos, has pictured in Jean Valjean a kind of big human beast who, when half awake, steals a loaf of bread to save others from starving, but who is startled into fullness of manhood by the sympathy and consideration of the good Bishop whose silver he had also stolen.

Hawthorne, in Donatello, has pictured a beautiful creature fully equipped with affections, emotions, passions, but with little consciousness of responsibility, until the fatal moment in which a crime illuminates his soul like a flash of lightning.

Such experiences are not to be compared with those of the prodigal son or of Saul. Before the one was reduced to husks, or the light blazed upon the other, they felt the obligation to do right. The prodigal chose pleasure with his eyes wide open and Saul was, mistakenly but truly, trying to do God's will even when he assisted in the stoning of Stephen.

Hugo, Goethe, and Hawthorne have accurately delineated single steps in the growth of the soul. They have shown how the process of the soul's awakening may be, and often has been, hastened. It may be hindered by false ideals and a vicious environment, and it may be hastened by lofty ideals and a holy environment.

Dr. Bushnell, in his lectures on Christian Nurture, has said that the formative years of every man's life are the first three. Is he correct? I am not sure, but there can be no doubt but what with a good environment the consciousness of moral obligation will be very early developed.

The soul cannot long be imprisoned. The consciousness of "ought" and "ought not" will break all barriers as a growing seed will split a rock; and, when that stage of growth appears, the soul knows itself.

When the soul is finally awakened, when it realizes that it is indissolubly bound to a larger personality in the unseen sphere; when it finds that it is tied to other souls, and that it cannot escape from its responsibility for itself and them, - what then? Then the struggle of life begins. The awakening is to a realization of conflict with the seen and unseen environment, with forces within and fascinations without. When Paul speaks of the law as the minister of death, he simply means that law introduces an ideal, and ideals always start struggles. Law is something to be obeyed. It is sure to antagonize the animal in man. When our possibilities dawn upon us, in that moment there comes the feeling that they should be our masters. Then the lower nature resists and becomes clamorous. Duty calls in one direction and inclination impels in another. The period of ignorance has passed. Weakness and imperfection remain, but not ignorance. There is a conflict in the soul. The law in the members wars against the law in the mind. We feel that we ought to move upward, but unseen weights press heavily upon us, and to rise seems impossible.

Between God calling from above and animalism from below the poor soul has a hard time of it. The morally great in all ages have become strong by overcoming their fleshly natures. They have risen on their dead selves to higher things. The vision of God has reached them even in their prison-houses; and it has broken their chains and they have begun to move toward Him. To the end of the chapter they have had a long fight, and not seldom have been sadly worsted. Goethe and Augustine, Pascal and Coleridge, DeQuincey and Webster - how the list of those who have had to fight bitter battles for spiritual liberty might be extended I and many have not been victorious before the shadows have lengthened and the day closed. Should they be blamed or pitied? Pitied, surely, and for the rest let us leave them to Him who knoweth all things. "Vengeance is mine; I will repay, saith the Lord." Men have nothing to do with judgment; the final word concerning any soul will be spoken only by Him whose vision is perfect. "Steep and craggy is the pathway of the gods," and steep and craggy is the path by which men rise to spiritual heights.

He who is sensitive to life can hardly survey this universal human struggle with undimmed eye or with unquestioning faith. The young are driven here and there by heartless and, sometimes, almost furious passions; some are weak and fall because they are blind, and others because they love and trust; and many who desire to do good mistake and choose evil. The strong often try to run away from themselves but can find no solitude in which to hide; and all the time right and truth shine in the darkness like stars. What shall we say of these confusing conditions? To ignore them is foolish; to insist that the struggle is but a delusion is nonsense. The only sane course is to face facts and adjust our theories to them.

The battle between duty and inclination, between the ideal and the actual, will continue as long as life in the body endures. It is not an unmixed evil. In the end right is never worsted. The way that leads to holiness is long and sometimes bloody; but it always develops strength and courage. The fight, for each individual, will be ended only by the full and perfect choice of truth and virtue, which are always the will of God. The victory will be secure long before it is fully won. Enough for us to know that conformity to the will of God at last will be the end of strife.

It is not well to be overmuch troubled when we see those whom we love fighting a hard battle against inherited tendencies and an evil environment, for the fight, however fierce, is a good sign. Those alone are to be pitied who are drifting, and not resisting. Progress is ever by a steep and spiral pathway. Sometimes the face of the ascending soul is toward the sun and sometimes it is toward the darkness. No man can deliver his friend from the forces which oppose him. Each must conquer for himself and none can evade the conflict. From the hour when the soul awakens to a consciousness of its powers and possibilities, its movement, in spite of all hindrances and difficulties, must be to the heights. Those only need cause anxiety who are not yet awake; or who, having been awake, have turned backward instead of pressing onward.

We are now face to face with a momentous inquiry. When the soul is awake, when it realizes something of its descent from God and of its relation to Him and to other souls, what should be its environment? Intelligent and otherwise sane people at this point have been strangely insane and blind. We are always affected by influence more than by teaching. Education by atmosphere is quite as effective as education by study. Involuntarily all become like their ideals. Personalities absorb characteristics from surroundings as flowers absorb colors from the light. The awakened soul, therefore, from the first should have a spiritual environment. Parents and friends should be helps, not hindrances, to its progress. I once read a letter from one who had changed an old for a new home. The letter was full of aspiration for the best things, of thoughts about God and the spiritual verities. It was not difficult to see that the new home in its reverence for truth, its loyalty to right, its reaching for reality, was providing the same good influence as the old one. If, in the environment, truth and duty are honored, virtue reverenced, God worshipped sincerely and devoutly, manhood held to be as sacred as deity, the unseen and spiritual never spoken of unadvisedly or lightly, courage always found hand in hand with character, the soul will never long fight a losing battle.

The home should be organized to promote, as swiftly as possible, the awakening of the souls of the children; and, from the moment of this awakening, everything should be planned to help their growth. The books on the tables should tell the life-stories of those who have bravely fought and never faltered.

Biographies of men like Wilberforce and Howard who have lived to help their fellow-men; and of women like Florence Nightingale and Lady Stanley, who have regarded their social gifts and ample wealth as calls to service; histories of charities, intellectual development and noble achievement, pictures like Sir Galahad and The Light of the World are potent forces in the formation of character. The ideal side of life should ever be presented in its most attractive form to the awakened soul in its near environment. Because the ideal culminates in the religious, and the feeling of moral obligation rests at last upon the conviction that God is, and that He is not far from any one, Jesus, in all the beauty and pathos of His earthly career, in all the tragic grandeur of His death and glory of His Resurrection, in all the nearness and helpfulness of His continuing ministry, should be the subject of frequent, earnest, honest, sane, and sympathetic conversation.

The awakened soul needs first of all an environment which will be favorable to its growth. Its development then will usually be steadily and swiftly toward God and conformity to His will. There ought to be no need of any re-awakening. If the soul opens its eyes among those who reverence truth and righteousness, who guard virtue and revere love, to whom God is the nearest and most blessed of realities, and Jesus is Master, Saviour, and daily Friend, its growth toward the spiritual goal will be as natural and beautiful as it will also be swift and sure.

THE FIRST STEPS

No mortal object did these eyes behold
When first they met the placid light of thine,
And my soul felt her destiny divine,
And hope of endless peace in me grew bold:
Heaven-born, the soul a heav'nward course must hold;
Beyond the visible world she soars to seek
(For what delights the sense is false and weak)
Ideal form, the universal mould.
The wise man, I affirm, can find no rest
In that which perishes: nor will he lend
His heart to aught which doth on time depend.
'Tis sense, unbridled will, and not true love,
Which kills the soul: Love betters what is best,
Even here below, but more in heaven above.

- Sonnet from Michael Angelo. Wordsworth

III

THE FIRST STEPS

The first movements of the awakened soul are difficult to trace. Observation, painstaking and long-continued, alone can furnish the desired information. In the attempt to recall our own experiences there is always a possibility of inaccuracy. Bias counts for more in self-examination than in an examination of others. There is also danger of confusing religious preconceptions with what actually transpires. What we have been led to imagine should be experienced we are very likely to insist has taken place. The truth concerning the Ascent of the Soul will be found in the conclusions of many observers in widely different conditions.

The soul awakens to a consciousness of its responsibilities and to a knowledge that it is in a moral order from which escape is forever impossible. This is our point of departure in this chapter.

The new-born child has to become adjusted to its physical environment, to learn to use its powers, to breathe, to eat, to allow the various senses to do their work. In like manner the newly awakened soul has to become adjusted to the moral order. The moral order is the rule of right in the sphere of thought, emotion, and choice. It is the government of the soul as the physical order is the government of the body. It may be best explained by analogy. There is a physical order ruled by physical laws. If those laws are obeyed, strength, health, sanity result; but if they are disobeyed, the consequences, which are inevitable and self-perpetuating, are weakness, disease, insanity. If one violates gravitation he is dashed in pieces; if he trifles with microbes their infinitesimal grasp will be like a shackle of steel. No one can get outside the physical universe and the sweep of its laws.

There is also a right and a wrong way to use thought, emotion, will. The mind which has hospitality only for holy thoughts will become clearer, and its vision more distinct; but the mind which harbors impure thoughts, gradually, but surely, confuses evil with good, obscures its vision, and becomes a fountain of moral miasm. If we choose to recall and to retain feelings that are animal, and are the relics of animalism, the natural tendency toward bestiality will gather momentum; but if emotion is turned toward higher objects, and we are thrilled from above rather than lulled from below, the sensibilities become sources of enduring joy. The moral order is like the physical order in its universality and in the remorselessness of the consequences which follow choices.

How does the soul become adjusted to the moral order? This question is difficult to answer. At the first there is sight enough to see that one course is right and another wrong, but the vision is indistinct. Gradually the ability to make accurate discriminations increases, and, with time and other growth, the faculty of vision is enlarged and clarified.

The first step in the Ascent of the Soul is the development of ability to discriminate between right and wrong. The powers of the soul are enlarged and vivified with the bodily growth, but whether there is any necessary connection between the growth of the one and that of the other, we know not. This alone is sure - clearer vision, with ever-increasing distinctness, reveals the certainty that moral laws are universal and unchangeable. The process of adjustment to the moral order is partly voluntary and partly involuntary. It is hastened by the hidden forces of vitality, and it may be hindered by its own choices. As a human being who refuses to eat will starve, so a soul which turns away from truth will starve. The law in one case is as inexorable as in the other. This consciousness of the moral order is sometimes dim even in mature years because neglect always deadens appreciation. Paul said that the law is a schoolmaster leading to Christ. By that he intended to teach that we must realize that we are under moral law before we can know that its violation will result in a state of ruin needing salvation. First that which is natural, then that which is spiritual. The phrase "natural law in the spiritual world" means that the consequences following right and wrong are as inevitable and essential in the realm of spirit as in that of matter.

The progress of the soul is dependent on the realization that there is a moral quality in thoughts, emotions, choices; that the consequences following them grow out of them as flowers from seed, and that they determine not only the character but the happiness and welfare of the one exercising them.

The next step in the upward movement of the soul is the realization of its freedom. It is possible for one to know that he is under law, without at the same time appreciating that he is free to choose whether he will obey. I may see a storm sweeping toward me and know that behind it is resistless force, and know, also, that to step outside the track of that storm is impossible; and it is conceivable that a soul may know itself as able to think, feel, act, and, at the same time, be under the dominion of forces before which it is powerless. The practical question, therefore, for all in this human world is not, are there spiritual laws? but, may we choose for ourselves whether we will obey or disobey them? Until the soul knows itself to be free to choose, there will be no deep feeling of obligation, without which there can be no motive impelling toward the heights. Here also we walk in the dark. The genesis of the consciousness of freedom has never been observed. DuBois-Reymond has called it one of "the seven riddles of science." We are no nearer the solution of the problem than were our fathers a thousand years ago. But one thing at least we do know: He who believes himself to be a puppet in the hands of unseen forces will never fight them. If freedom is a fiction the universe is not only unmoral, but immoral. The final argument for freedom is consciousness. I know I could have chosen differently from what I did. But how do I know? The process cannot be pushed farther back. Consciousness is ultimate and authoritative. But what then shall be said of heredity? A child when first born is little but a bundle of sensibilities. Its growth seems to be but the unfolding of inherited tendencies. Every man is what his ancestors have made him plus what he has absorbed from his environment. How can we say then that any are free? That man who is surly, uncomfortable, ugly, as hard to endure as a March wind, is but the extension of his father. When one knows the elder it is difficult to do otherwise than pity the younger. He is but living the tendencies which were born in him and which are an inseparable part of his nature. He cannot be genial and urbane. Are not some born moral cripples as others are born with physical deformities? Are not some spiritually deaf, dumb, and blind from birth? It cannot be doubted. We are all more or less what our fathers were, but our surroundings do much to modify us. Many men seem to be driven on wings of passion, as leaves by tornadoes; and yet we know that we are free, and that all life and conduct, individual and social, must be ordered on that hypothesis. Teach men that they are not free, and anarchy and chaos will quickly follow. No freedom? Then there is no obligation. No one feels that he ought to do what he cannot do, and no one will try to do what he does not feel that he ought to do. If men are but machines, moving only as the power is turned on, there is no moral quality in any action. If we live in a moral world, whether we can understand it or not, we must be free to choose for ourselves. The possibility of the soul's expansion depends on its freedom. There is no right and no wrong, no truth and no error, if it is a slave to the inheritance with which it was born. What gives to the invitations of Jesus a quality so serious and so solemn is the fact that they may be rejected. The power of choice is the most sublime endowment which man possesses. When we have learned to know ourselves as free a long step forward has been taken. The soul grows by a right use of the power of choice.

How may it be adjusted to this knowledge? It will undoubtedly grow to it, but the process will be slow. It may, however, be hastened by a use of the experience of others. No man should be allowed to begin the battle of life as ignorant as his father was. Each new soul should have the benefit of the experience of all who have lived before. Children should be taught by example and conversation, in the home and the school, that the beginning of wisdom is a right use of the experience of others. However this lesson may be learned, and however swift may be the process of growth, the next step in the soul's progress, after its realization that it is in a moral order, must be its adjustment to the fact that it is a free agent and sovereign over its own choices.

No man is ever forced into any course of conduct. Character is the resultant of many choices rather than of necessity. The moral law may be obeyed or it may be violated. Its seat is, indeed, in the bosom of God. It is the only guarantee of individual progress and social harmony. Its sway is without bound and without end. To know how to live in a moral world, and how best to use the gifts of liberty, is a subject for an eternity of study. That this consciousness of freedom comes slowly is an immense blessing; otherwise the soul would be dazed as, for the first time, it looked around on the solemnities and splendors of the spiritual universe; and be overwhelmed as it realized, at the very beginning of its career, that it was endowed with a sovereignty as mysterious and potent as that of God.

The next step in the upward movement of the soul is appreciation of a moral ideal. That is a solemn and sublime moment when the newly awakened soul realizes that it dwells in a moral order and is free to make its own choices. But another moment is equally thrilling - that in which, in faint and scarcely audible accents, it catches the far call of the goal toward which, henceforward and forever, it must move. It now knows not only that there is a difference between right and wrong, but that there are mysterious affinities between itself and truth and right. Later the sound of that far-away voice will become more distinct. But in its infancy the soul is more or less confused. It hears many sounds and does not always know how to distinguish between siren voices and those which prophesy its destiny. It also has to learn to distinguish truth and right. The task of making moral discriminations is not easy at any time. Amid a babel of noises to detect the one clear call which alone can satisfy is almost impossible. The mistakes, therefore, are many, but even by mistakes the soul learns to distinguish the true from the false. But how is it to be taught to appreciate that one voice only in all that confusion of strange sounds should be heeded, and all the rest disregarded? The same answer as before must be given. This knowledge, also, will come in large part with the years. It seems to be the cosmic purpose to provide fresh light with every new step of progress. No one is ever left in total darkness. As the soul advances it learns to distinguish between the voices which speak to it. The necessity of growth is the angel of the Lord whose ministries and prophecies are the hope and glory of the race. Growth may be hindered, but it can never be banished from the universe. It moved in chaos, and never faltered in its march, until under its beneficent leading all things were seen to be good. It led the cosmic movement until man appeared; and now it has taken man in hand, with all the vestiges of animalism clinging to him, and it will never leave him as he rises toward the perfection and glory of God. The law of growth answers most if not all of our questions. The soul of man must grow. With its growth will come vision, strength, and progress toward its goal.

But growth is not all. The voices to which we choose to give heed will sound most distinctly in our ears. Here we face a fact which is often in evidence. The earth and animalism will never cease to make appeal to our senses, while at the same time voices from above will call from their heights to our spirits. To distinguish between desire and duty, between truth and tradition, between the spiritual and the animal, is a step which has to be taken, and which is taken whether we appreciate how or not. By the pain which follows wrong choices, or by the intuitions of the spirit, the soul comes to realize that its obligation is always in one direction; that its choice ought to be in favor of the morally excellent. But how shall it discern the morally excellent? The process of learning will be a long one, and never fully completed on the earth. This is a realm that poets and dramatists, who are usually the profoundest and most accurate students of life, have not often tried to enter. Such questions can be answered only after careful and long-continued inductive study. Moralists are usually content to stop short of this inquiry. How the soul comes to learn that it is obligated to truth and right we may not fully know; but that it does learn, and that no step in all its development is more important, there is no doubt. In His dealing with this question Jesus preserves the same attitude as toward all subjects of speculation. I came not to explain how life adjusts itself to its environment, He seems to say, but to give life a richness and a beauty which it never had before; I came not to answer questions, but to save to the best uses that which already exists. Nevertheless, the question as to how the soul is taught to distinguish the morally excellent is of serious importance. If we do not recognize the sanctity of truth and right we may not give them hospitality; and we may not appreciate their sanctity if we are ignorant of what gives them their authority. How, then, does it learn what truth and right are? Are there any clearly defined paths by which this knowledge may be reached? Is not truth a matter of education? And is there any absolute right? A Hindoo Swami, of the school of the Vedanta, lecturing in this country, solemnly assured an intelligent audience that there is no sin; that what is called sin is only the result of education; that what is vice in one place may be virtue in another; and that in the sphere of morals all is relative and nothing absolute. Then there is no wrong, for wrong and sin are closely related; and no right because if right is not a dream it implies the possibility of an opposite. There is little permanent danger from such shallow theories. The peril from confusion is greater than from denial. But even confusion at this point is not long necessary because in every soul there is a voice which men call conscience, which never fails to impel toward the true and the good. Conscience may be likened to a compass whose needle always points toward the north. When it is uninfluenced by distracting causes conscience always shows the way toward truth and right. The Spartans believed that lying was a virtue if it was sufficiently obscure; and a Hindoo woman who throws her child to the god of the Ganges does so because she is deeply religious. Are not such persons conscientious? Yet they perform acts which are in themselves wrong? Of what value, then, is conscience? That they are both conscientious and religious I have no doubt. It is their misfortune to be ignorant. The light appears to be colored by the medium through which it passes, and yet it is not colored; and conscience seems to approve what is wrong, and yet it never does. It always impels toward the right, but men often make serious mistakes because of their ignorance. The needle in the moral compass is deflected by selfishness or false teaching. The Hindoo mother might hear and, if she dared to listen to it, would hear a deeper voice than the one calling her to sacrifice her child - even one telling her to spare her child. She has not yet learned that it is always safe to trust the moral sense. Superstitions are not conscience; they are ignorance obscuring and deadening conscience. Every man is born with a guide within to point him to paths of virtue and truth, and one of the most important lessons which the growing soul has to learn is that when it is true to itself it may always trust that guide. The call of his destiny finds every man, and, when he hears it, he asks: How may I reach that goal? It is far away and the path is confused. Then a voice within makes answer, and, if he heeds that, he will make no mistake. That voice, I believe, is the result of no evolutionary process, but is the holy God immanent in every soul, making His will known. Evolution gradually gives to conscience a larger place, but there is no evidence that it is produced by any physical process. It may be hindered by physical limitations, but it can be destroyed by none. Why are we so slow in learning that conscience, being divine, is authoritative and may be trusted? I know no answer except this: We so often confuse ignorance with conscience that at last we conclude that the latter is not trustworthy. But there we mistake. It is trustworthy. It never fails those who heed its message. That realization may now and then come early, but it seldom comes all at once. Nevertheless it is a step to be taken before the progress of the soul can be either swift or sure.

The moment that the soul realizes that God is not far away, but within; that all the divine voices did not speak in the past, but that many are speaking now; that whosoever will listen may hear within his own being a message as clear and sacred as any that ever came to prophet or teacher in other times, it will begin to realize the luxury of its liberty, and something of the grandeur of its destiny. Truth and right are not fictions of the imagination, they are realities opening before the growing soul like continents before explorers. They always invite entrance and possession. They have horizons full of splendor and beauty and music. They alone can satisfy. But the soul has not yet fully escaped from the mists and fogs and glooms of the earth. It is surrounded by those who still wallow in animalism, and the sounds of the lower world are yet echoing in its ears. But at last its face is toward the light; the far call of its destiny has been heard; it knows itself to be in a moral order; it is assured that, however closely the body may be imprisoned, no bolts and no bars can shut in a spirit; that before it is a fair and favored land, far off but ever open; and, best of all, that within its own being, impervious to all influences from without, is a guide which may be implicitly trusted and which will never betray. Why not follow its suggestions at once and press on toward that fair land of truth and beauty which so earnestly invites? Ah! why not? Here we are face to face with other facts. There are hindrances, many and serious, in the pathway of the soul, and they must be met and forced before that land can be entered. This is the time for us to consider them.

HINDRANCES

And many, many are the souls
Life's movement fascinates, controls;
It draws them on, they cannot save
Their feet from its alluring wave;
They cannot leave it, they must go
With its unconquerable flow;

*   *   *   *   *

They faint, they stagger to and fro,
And wandering from the stream they go;
In pain, in terror, in distress,
They see all round a wilderness.

- Epilogue to Lessing's "Laocoon". Matthew Arnold

IV

HINDRANCES

When the soul has heard the far call of its destiny and realizes that it may respond to that call, and that it has, in conscience, a guide which will not fail even in the deepest darkness, it turns in the direction from which the appeal comes and begins to move toward its goal. Almost simultaneously it realizes that it has to meet and to overcome numerous and serious obstacles. To the hindrances in the way of the spirit our thought is to be turned in this chapter.

The moral failure of many men and women of superb intellectual and physical equipment is one of the sad and serious marvels of human history. What a pathetic and significant roll might be made of those who have been great intellectually and pitiful failures morally! It has often been affirmed that Hannibal might have conquered Rome, and been the master of the world except for the fatal winter at Capua. Antony, possibly, would have been victor at Actium if it had not been for something in himself that made him susceptible to the fascination of the fair but treacherous Egyptian queen. Achilles was a symbolical as well as an historical character. There was one place - with him in the heel - where he was vulnerable, and through that he fell. Socrates was like a tornado when inflamed by anger. Napoleon laid Europe waste and desolated more distant lands, but he was an enormous egotist and morally a blot on civilization.

The life-history of many of the poets is inexpressibly sad. Chatterton, Shelley, Byron, Poe - their very names call up facts which those who admire their genius would gladly conceal. Many artists are in the same category. It explains nothing to ascribe their moral pollution to their finer sensibilities, for finer sensibilities ought to be attended by untarnished characters. It is, perhaps, best not even to mention their names lest, thereby, we dull the appreciation of noble masterpieces which represent the better moods of the men. One of imperial genius was a slave to wine, another to lust, another was too envious to detect any merit in the work of others of his craft. There are statesmen of whose achievements we speak, but never of the men themselves; and there have been ministers of the Gospel, unhappily not a few, who have suddenly disappeared and been heard of no more. Into a kindly oblivion they have gone, and that is all that any one needs to know. What do such facts signify? That many, or most, of these men have been essentially and totally bad? Or that they are moral failures? They signify only that they have not yet risen above the hindrances which they have found in their pathways. The world knows of the temporary obscuration of a fair fame; it does not see the grief, the tears, the gradual gathering of the energies for a new assault upon the obstacles in the road; and it does not see how tenderly, but faithfully, Providence, through nature, is dealing with them. Some time they will be brought to themselves - The Eternal Goodness is the pledge of that. It is not with this unseen and beneficent ministry of restoration, however, that I am now dealing, but with the awful wrecks and failures which are so common in human history, and concerning which most men know something in their own experiences. How shall they be explained? - since to evade them is impossible. In other words when a man is awake, when he feels that he is in a moral order, is free, and hears the call of his destiny, why is his progress so slow and difficult? No one has ever delineated this period in the soul's growth with greater vividness than Bunyan. The Valley of Humiliation, the Slough of Despond, Giant Despair, Doubting Castle are all pictures of human life taken with photographic accuracy. What are some of these hindrances?

Amory H. Bradford

The soul is free, but its abode is in a limited body. The movement of the soul is swift and unconstrained as thought. It is not limited by time. It may project itself a thousand years into the future or travel a thousand years into the past; but it dwells in the body and is more or less restrained by it. Bodily limitation narrows experience and compels ignorance. It makes large acquaintance impossible. The flowers beneath the ice on the Alps are small; the flowers of the tropics have the proportions of trees. Thus environment modifies growth. The body cannot put fetters on the will, but it may hold in captivity the powers which acquire knowledge, withhold from the emotions persons worthy of affection, and make the range of objects of choice poor and pitiful. The soul has often been compared to a bird in a cage, - fitted for broad horizons but confined within narrow spaces. This hindrance is a very real one. The man who grows swiftly must be in the open world with beings to love and to serve ever within his reach. Hence the life beyond death is often called the unhindered life because of its freedom from the body. The old story of "Rasselas" is symbolical. In the Happy Valley a man might be as good, but he could not be as great and wise, as in the larger world. The soul will meet fewer temptations there, but those it does encounter will be more insistent and harder to escape. He who would respond to a call to service must needs have about him those whom he may serve. Large views are for those who are able to rise to the heights. He who lives in a cave may be true to his little light, and surely is responsible for no more, but he will see far less than the one whose home is on the mountaintop. Thus even bodily limitations, to which are attached no moral qualities, are hindrances to the growth of the being, whose destiny is not only purification but expansion: - its movement is not only toward goodness but also toward greatness; not only toward virtue but also toward power.

The animal entail is one of the greatest mysteries of our mortal life. The soul in its moments of illumination feels that it is related to some person like itself, but far higher, and aspires to it. Sir Joshua Reynolds' figure of "Faith" in the famous window in the chapel of New College, Oxford, suggests the attitude of the newly awakened soul. In freshness and beauty it is turning toward the light. But in human experience something occurs which Sir Joshua has not tried to depict. A clammy hand reaches up from the deeps out of which rise suffocating clouds, and that pure spirit finds itself enveloped in darkness and fastened to the earth. The humiliation is complete. What has occurred? Only what has happened again and again; and what will continue to happen for no one knows how long. The animal has gotten the better of the spirit. The soul has sinned - for sin is little, if anything, but a spirit allowing itself to return to the fascinations of the animal conditions out of which it has been evolved, and from which it ought to have escaped forever. The animal entail is the chief hindrance to the aspiring spirit. The animal lives by his senses. He is content when they are satisfied. It can hardly be said that animals are ever happy. Happiness is a state higher than contentment. Paul said he had learned in whatsoever state he was to be content, but even he never said that in all states he had learned to be happy. Animals are contented when their senses are gratified and they are savage when their senses are clamorous. Lions and bears are dangerous when they are hungry, and cruel when other desires are obstructed.

Whatever the theory of evolution, from the beginning of its upward movement, the nearest, most potent, and most dangerous hindrance to the soul is this entail of animalism, which it can never escape but which it must some time conquer. The spirit and the body seem to be in endless antagonism, and yet the body itself will become the fair servant of the soul when once the question of its supremacy has been determined. The tendency to revert to animalism has been vividly depicted by the poets, and the clamorous and insistent nature of the passions portrayed by the artists.

The liquor in the enchanted cup of Comus may be called "the wine of the senses." Its effect is thus described by Milton. Comus offers

... "To every weary traveler
His orient liquor in a crystal glass,
To quench the drought of Phoebus; which, as they taste
(For most do taste through fond, intemperate thirst)
Soon as the potion works, their human countenance,
The express resemblance of the gods, is changed
Into some brutish form of wolf or bear,
Or ounce or tiger, hog or bearded goat."

A famous passage from Ovid's "Metamorphoses"[4] represents Actaeon as changed into a stag; but, if I read the fable aright, the glimpse of Diana in her bath, while not an intelligent choice, was more than a mere accident - it was the uprising of innate sensuality; for even the Greek gods were supposed to have had senses.

[Footnote 4: Addison's translation, Book III, pages 188-198.]

"Actaeon was the first of all his race,
Who grieved his grandsire in his borrowed face;
Condemned by stern Diana to bemoan
The branching horns and visage not his own;
To shun his once-loved dogs, to bound away
And from their huntsman to become their prey;
And yet consider why the change was wrought;
You'll find it his misfortune, not his fault;
Or, if a fault it was the fault of chance;
For how can guilt proceed from ignorance?"

The story of Circe is the common story of those who have yielded to the flesh. The companions of Ulysses visited the palace of Circe, were allured by her charms, and the result is read in these words:

"Before the spacious front, a herd we find
Of beasts, the fiercest of the savage kind.
Our trembling steps with blandishments they meet
And fawn, unlike their species, at our feet."

The strong words of Milton are none too strong:

"Their human countenance
The express resemblance of the gods, is changed
Into some brutish form."

A common subject with artists has been the temptations of the saints. They have fled from luxury, and what they supposed to be moral peril, but have found no solitude to which they could go and leave their bodies behind. In the silences faces have appeared to them full of alluring entreaty, and more than one anchorite has found to his sorrow that he carried within himself the cause of his danger.

A singularly vivid painting represents one of the saints in the desert, and clinging to him, with their arms around his neck, are two figures of exquisite physical beauty. Their charms are so near and perilous that the pale and haggard man in desperation has shut his eyes, and in this extremity, with his one free hand, is frantically clinging to a cross. The artist has accurately depicted the condition in which the soul finds itself as it begins its growth; - its chief enemies are those of its own household.

Happy indeed is it for all that none see at the first the obstacles in their way. Faint and far shines the splendor of the goal; the hindrances are reached one by one, and each one, for the moment, seems to be the last.

But close and persistent as is the animal entail, it is not unconquerable. Many a Sir Galahad, and many a woman fair and holy as his pure sister, have lived on this earth of ours. They were not always so; and their beauty and holiness are but the outshining of spiritual victory.

Is this environment of evil necessary to the development of the soul? We may not know; but we do know that it can be conquered, and some time and somehow will be conquered; and that then men, like ourselves, grown from the same stock, evolved from the lower levels, will constitute "the crowning race."

"No longer half akin to brute,
For all we thought and loved and did,
And hoped, and suffered, is but seed
Of what in them is flower and fruit."

These are a few samples of the hindrances which the soul must face in its progress through "the thicket of this world." But these are not all. Hardly less serious is the ignorance which clothes it like a garment. It comes it knows not whence; it journeys it knows not whither, and apparently is attended by no one wiser than itself.

Hugo's awful picture of a man in the ocean with the vast and silent heavens above, the desolate waves around, the birds like dwellers from another world circling in the evening light, and the poor fellow trying to swim, he knows not where, is not so wide of the mark as some thoughtless readers might suppose.

The soul is ignorant and timid, in the vast and void night, with its environment of ignorance and of other souls also blindly struggling. At the same time there is the consciousness of a duty to do something, of a voice calling it somewhere which ought to be heeded, and of having bitterly failed.

The solitariness of the soul is also one of the most mysterious and solemn of its characteristics. The prophecy which is applied to Jesus might equally be applied to every human being: He trod the wine-press alone. In all its deepest experiences the soul is solitary. Craving companionship, in the very times when it seeks it most it finds it denied. Every crucial choice must at last be individual. When sorrows are multiplied there are in them deeps into which no friendly eye can look. When the hour of death comes, even though friends crowd the rooms, not one of them can accompany the soul on its journey. It seems as if this solitariness must hinder its growth. Perhaps were our eyes clearer we should see that what seems to retard in reality hastens progress. But to our human sight it seems as if every soul needed companionship and cooeeperation in all its deep experiences; and that the ancients were not altogether wrong in their belief in the presence and protection of Guardian Angels. But something more vital and assuring than that faith is desired. It is rather the inseparable fellowship of those who are facing the same mysteries and fighting the same battles as ourselves; but even that not infrequently is denied.

Is this all? There is another possibility which observation has never detected and which science is powerless to disprove. Can we be sure that no malign spiritual influences hinder and bewilder? We cannot be sure. The common belief of nearly all peoples ought not to be rudely brushed aside. No one willingly believes in lies nor clings to them when he knows that they are lies. Superstitions always have some element of truth in them, and the truth, not the error, wins adherents. The most that we can say, at this point, is that we do not know. It is possible that the common beliefs of many widely separated people have no basis in fact, that they are born of dreams and delusions; and, on the other hand, it is equally possible that the spaces which we inhabit, but which we cannot fully explore, have other inhabitants than our vision discerns, and that those beings may help and may hinder us in our progress. It is not wise to dogmatize where we are ignorant. While the scales balance we must wait.

Are the hindrances in the path of the soul without any ministry? That cannot be; for then they are exceptions to the universal law, that nothing which exists is without a purpose of benefit.

All the analogies of nature indicate that human limitations are intended to serve some good end, since, so far as observation has yet extended, it has found nothing which is caused by chance. Emerson says, "As the Sandwich Islander believes that the strength and valor of the enemy he kills passes into himself, so we gain the strength of the temptations we resist;"[5] and

St. Bernard says, "Nothing can work me damage except myself; the harm that I sustain I carry about with me, and never am a real sufferer but by my own fault."[6]

[Footnote 5: Essay on Compensation.]

[Footnote 6: Quoted by Emerson in Essay on Compensation.]

And St. John says, "To him that overcometh will I give to eat of the tree of life."[7]

[Footnote 7: Revelation 2:7.]

The mission of the austere is the development of strength. Concerning this suggestion we shall inquire later. The souls which have reached the serene summits have ever been those which have most resolutely faced the obstacles in their pathways. Even apparent hindrances always exercise a beneficent ministry. As Jesus was made perfect by the things which He suffered, so, in the Cosmic plan, all souls must come to strength and perfection by the difficulties which they overcome and the enemies which they subdue.

What should be the attitude of the soul in view of the hindrances by which it is environed? It should be taught to fight them at every point. Nowhere is the kindness of nature more evident than in the patience and persistence with which this instruction is conveyed.

Nature withholds her favors until they are earned. New light comes only to those who have used-the light they had. Strength is developed by resistance. Growth is for those who place themselves where growth is possible. Nature gives the soul nothing, but she always waits to cooeperate with it. This lesson was impressed long ago. It ought never to require new emphasis. Let the younger study the experiences of their elders. They will be saved many failures and much pain. The soul can never be coerced, but it may be taught. Milton has enforced this great lesson in Comus:

"Against the threats
Of malice or of sorcery, of that power
Which erring men call Chance, this I hold firm -
Virtue may be assailed, but never hurt,
Surprised by unjust force, but not enthralled;
Yet, even that which mischief meant most harm,
Shall in the happy trial prove most glory;
But evil on itself shall back recoil,
And mix no more with goodness, when at last
Gathered like a scum, and settled to itself,
It shall be in eternal restless change
Self-fed, and self-consumed; if this fail
The pillar'd firmament is rottenness
And earth's base built on stubble."

No one should believe, after all the growth of the ages, that the soul was made to be imprisoned in a fleshly prison. It was intended that it should burst its barriers and press toward the light. There is an eternal enmity between the serpent and the soul, and the serpent's head must be bruised, but the soul resisting all the forces and fascinations of the flesh, rising on that which has been cast down to higher things, slowly but surely, painfully but with ever added strength moves toward the ideal humanity which has never been better defined than as "the fullness of Christ."

Meanwhile it is well to reinforce our faith by remembering that it is written in the nature of things that truth and goodness must prevail.

This is a moral universe. Error never can be victorious. It may be exalted for a time, but that will be only in order that it may be sunk to deeper depths. Evil and error are doomed and always have been. Evil is moral disease, and disease always tends toward death, while life always and of necessity presses toward larger, more beautiful, and more beneficent being.

Here let us rest. Many things are dark and impossible of explanation, but we have already been taught a few lessons of superlative importance. We have learned that the soul is made for the light; that it can be satisfied only with love and truth; that every hindrance may be overcome; that the animal was made to be the servant of the spirit; that the body makes a good servant but a poor master; that strength comes to those who refuse to submit to the clamors of appetite: thus we have been led to see something of the way along which the soul has moved from animalism toward freedom and victory.

And we have learned one thing more, viz., that the Over-soul is not a dream, but a reality; that the individual may be in correspondence with the Over-soul and from it be continually reinforced. Or, to put our faith in sweeter and simpler form, we have learned by experience which cannot be gainsaid that God is a personal spirit, interested in all that concerns His children, and anxious for their growth; and that He can no more allow His love for them to be defeated than He could allow the suns and planets to break from their orbits. How much more is a man than a sun! Therefore, since God is in His heaven, all must be right with the world and with man, and some time all the hindrances will be changed into helps, all obstacles be converted into strength, and "all hells into benefit."

THE AUSTERE

We cannot kindle when we will
The fire which in the heart resides;
The Spirit bloweth and is still,
In mystery our soul abides.
But tasks in hours of insight will'd
Can be through hours of gloom fulfill'd.

With aching hands and bleeding feet
We dig and heap, lay stone on stone;
We bear the burden and the heat
Of the long day, and wish 'twere done.
Not till the hours of light return,
All we have built do we discern.

- *Morality.* Matthew Arnold.

V

THE AUSTERE

The soul has discovered that it is in a moral order, that it is a free agent, and that it has mysterious affinities with truth and right. It has taken a few steps, and with them has learned that its upward movement will not be easy.

It next discovers that it has no isolated existence, but that it is surrounded by countless other similar beings all indissolubly bound together and having mutual relations. With the dawn of intelligence comes the realization of relations. This realization is dim at the first, but it is very real. Soon the soul learns that the relations between it and other souls are so intimate that the interest of one is the interest of all. Appreciation of relations is a long advance in the movement upward, and it necessitates other knowledge. The realization of relations leads, necessarily and swiftly, to the consciousness of responsibility. The process of this growth cannot be described in detail, but the path is clearly marked and its milestones may be numbered. Each soul is always in a society of souls. Each one, therefore, affects others, and is affected by them. It is free and, therefore, responsible for the influence which it exerts. Moreover, it is bound to other souls by love, and love always carries with it the possibility of sorrow; for sorrow is usually only love thwarted. It is not far from the truth to say that when there is no love there is no sorrow, and that the possibilities of sorrow are always increased in proportion to the perfection of being.

In time the soul finds itself not only one among myriads of souls, but it realizes that its relations to some are more intimate than to others. It needs not to seek the causes of this fact, since it cannot escape from the reality. Thus it finds itself in families, in tribes, in nations, in social groups where the bonds are strong and enduring.

Some souls, more capacious than others, have a richer and more varied experience, and thus inevitably become teachers. The process goes on, and, with both teachers and scholars, the horizon expands and the strength increases with each new day. The soul has found that it is not a solitary being dazed and saddened by the consciousness of its powers, but that it is in a society in which all are similarly endowed, and that all are pressing toward the same goal. It has discovered that its growth is hastened, or hindered, by its environment; and that the spiritual environment is ever the nearest and most potent.

Each new step in this pilgrim's progress reveals something more wonderful than the opening of a continent. It is an entrance into a larger and more complex world. A strange fact now emerges. Every enlargement of being, either of faculty or capacity, is attended by pain either physical or mental. "Whom the Lord loveth He chasteneth," seems to be a universal law rather than an isolated text. All life is strenuous because it is always attended by growth. The soul moves not only onward but upward, and climbing is always a difficult process.

Before a second step is taken the soul begins to experience suffering and sorrow; and as its growth advances it never afterward, so far as human sight has penetrated, escapes from them. Why are they allowed? And what purpose do they serve?

The soul exists in a body, and the body is the seat of sensations. Those sensations, whether pleasing or painful, belong to the physical organs, but they affect the spirit, and escape from them is impossible. Pain has a perceptible effect on the soul, even though the latter has no other relation to the body than that of tenant to a house. It suffers because of the intimate relations which it sustains to the organs through which it works.

The individual soul is related to other souls. Therefore it has plans and purposes concerning them, and it has affinities which are inseparable from existence in society. Those purposes and affinities may be gratified or thwarted. The soul sometimes finds a response from the one whom it seeks and sometimes it does not. Pain belongs to the body, and sorrow is an experience of the soul.

The body is in constant limitations, subject to diseases and accidents, and the soul is affected by all that the body feels. Because of these intimate relationships the soul is limited by ignorance, and defeated in its purposes. It becomes attached to other souls, and those attachments are either rudely shattered or roughly repulsed, and, consequently, the life of the soul is as full of sorrow as is a summer day of clouds.

It faces its hindrances and rises by overcoming them. It finds pain besetting nearly every step of its advance, and the constant shadow of its existence is sorrow. Along such a pathway it moves in its ascent and, in spite of all opposition, it is never permanently hindered; while sorrow and suffering continually add to its strength. The austere experiences through which all pass hasten their spiritual growth. They are ever ministers of blessing; they pay no visits without leaving some fair gifts behind.

Questions arise here which it is difficult to answer. Why are such ministries needed? Why could not the ascent of the spirit be along an easier pathway? Why should it be necessary to write its history in tears and blood? Inquiries like these are insistent. Optimism assumes that the end always justifies the means, even when we are in the dark as to why other means were not used; and that it is better to comfort ourselves with the beneficent fact than to refuse to be comforted because we may not penetrate the depths of the Cosmic process. The emphasis of thought may well rest here. The austere is never merely the severe. What seems to human sight to be evil and only evil, always has a side of benefit. The soul is purified and strengthened as it rises above animalism; it is made courageous by bodily pain; tears clarify its vision. Even Jesus is said to have been made perfect by the things which He suffered. The universal characteristic of life is growth, and growth ever reaches out of old and narrow toward new, larger and better environment.

The soul needs strength, vision, sympathy, faith. These qualities are the fruit of experience. Muscle is converted into strength by use; and its use is possible only as it finds something to overcome. Vision is largely the fruit of training. The man on the lookout discovers a ship ahead long before the passenger on the deck. That fine accuracy of sight has come to him as he has battled with the tempests, and learned to distinguish between the whiteness of flying foam and the sunlight on a sail. Clearness of spiritual vision is acquired in the same way. He who can see even to "the far-off interest of tears" has been taught his discernment by reading the meaning of nearer events.

Sympathy is the art of suffering with another without the definite choice to do so. One soul spontaneously enters into the condition of another and bears his pains and griefs as though they were his own; that is sympathy. But who ever bore the griefs of another before he himself had felt sadness? Sympathy is a fruit that grows on the tree of sorrow. So intensely is this felt that even kindly words in hours of deep trial are ungrateful if they come from one who had had no hard experience of his own. In proportion as one has borne his own griefs he is presumed to be able to bear the griefs of others. He who has passed through the valley of the shadow, and who knows the way, is the only one whose hand is sought by another approaching the same valley. No human characteristic is more beautiful, or more appreciated, than sympathy; but its genuineness is seldom trusted unless the one offering it is known to have suffered himself.

Amory H. Bradford

Jesus is said to have been a man of sorrows and acquainted with grief, and, therefore, has led the long procession of the broken-hearted toward hope and peace. There is no other place known among men for the cultivation of sympathy except the school of suffering.

If possible, faith even more than sympathy is dependent on struggle. There is no other conceivable means by which it can be acquired. It cannot be imparted. No multiplying of words increases faith. If one has been in the blackest darkness and some way, he knows not how, has been led out into light, it will be easier for him to think that the same experience may be realized again. If every sorrow has had in it some hidden seed of blessing; if the overcoming of hindrances has ever increased strength; if at the very moment that calamity seemed ready to destroy the storm has blown around, and this has occurred again and again, it is impossible to refrain from expecting, or at least hoping, that behind the darkness an unseen hand is making things to work for good. Faith is essential to courage. He never cares to struggle who knows that failure is just ahead. Courage is required as the soul progresses, and becomes more deeply conscious of the mysteries and enemies by which it is surrounded. Faith results from the experience of beneficent leading. If one has been guided by love through many periods, and if that love has always been found waiting for its object on every corner of life, it will, ere long, be expected, watched for, and trusted.

Strength, vision, sympathy, courage, the fair attributes of the soul, all appear as it overcomes difficulties, fights doubts, goes deep into sorrow, and thus learns to realize that it is being led. It is easy to see how sorrow, pain, and death in the older legends and poetry were so often spoken of as beneficent angels. They are like those Sisters of Charity who hide beneath their long black bonnets serene and angelic faces. The austere in human life has never yet been explained, but it has been justified millions of times, and will be justified every time a human soul rises toward the goal for which all were created and toward which all, slowly or swiftly, are moving.

These conclusions have many confirmations, and with some of them it will be worth while to spend a little time. Every thinking man's experience assures him that he grows by overcoming. Emerson has finely said that we have occasion to thank our faults, by which he means limitations; and he has also reminded us that the oyster mends its broken shell with pearl.

We do not like overmuch to read with care our own experiences; but, when we are honest, we see that every struggle has left a residuum of added strength, that every loss has been a gain, that every calamity has opened doors into a larger world, and that what has been dreaded most has really most enriched us. Experience is a wise teacher.

History confirms the witness of experience. The strong man has always gained strength by struggle. The story of a few of the preeminent teachers is impressive reading. Mahomet knew the bitter pangs of poverty; Epictetus was a slave; Socrates was regarded as a fanatic, if not a lunatic, by most of the people of Athens; Siddhartha is said to have been a useless and luxurious young man until, wearied with the monotony of his father's palace, he ventured into the larger world and saw wherever he went poverty, sickness, death. He was startled into activity by the want, woe, and misery through which his pathway led.

Nearly all moral and spiritual leaders have had to suffer and thus grow strong. Mere genius has done little for human progress. It has made physical discoveries, but seldom touched the sphere of the soul. Elijah heard the voice of God in the midst of the terrors of the wilderness in which he was ready to die; Isaiah shared the usual fate of reformers and spoke his message into the ears of those who returned insult for warning. The story of Job is a long tragedy, - the world's tragedy, the tragedy of the soul in all ages. What deeps of anguish Dante fathomed before he could begin to write! Who can read the story of "Faust," as Goethe has interpreted it, without feeling that in it he has given the world in thin disguise much of his own life-story? Shakespeare alone, of men of genius of the first rank, seems to have learned comparatively few of his lessons in the school of suffering. But, possibly, if more were known of Shakespeare, it would be found that Lear, Macbeth, and Hamlet are but the expressions of lessons learned as he fought life's battle.

The "In Memoriam" of Tennyson, the "De Profundis" of Mrs. Browning, and the rich and glorious music of Robert Browning could have come only from souls which had been profoundly moved by grief and pain. All men listen most attentively to those who have gone farthest into the dark shadows.

The austere in human experience always accomplishes a purpose of blessing; and the soul comes into such an environment, not for the purpose of being humiliated, but in order that its strength may be developed, its sight clarified, and its powers perfected.

Thus we reach a rational basis for optimism. It has been said that optimism must not only show that beneficent results are being accomplished in human life, but it must also justify the means by which such results are achieved. It is not enough to show that all will be well in the end; it must be shown that even grief, pain, loss, and death are ordained to be the servants of man. This is evident to all who allow themselves to reach to the deeper meanings of their limitations and sufferings.

Opposite conclusions have been reached by some of those who have studied the hard and harsh phenomena of human life. The dreamy Hindu mind at first seemed to discern the truth that suffering is but the under side of blessing, and the hymns of the Vedas are full of hope and anticipation of better times; but, under the stress of prolonged disappointment and measureless calamities, bewildered in his attempt to explain the mystery of suffering, the Hindu at last came to deny its reality. But no bitter trials can be escaped by denial, and in India, to-day, disappointment and calamity are no less frequent than in elder ages. Refusal to believe in darkness effects no change in a midnight. The negation of precipices makes the ascent of a mountain no easier, and the denial of sickness, sorrow, and death deliver none from their presence. On the other hand, the very rocks that are the most difficult to scale will lift the climber toward an ampler horizon; and he who places his feet upon his temptations and sorrows will see in his own life the increasing purpose that widens with the suns.

Slowly, and over many obstacles, the soul rises from its humiliation and presses toward the heights, and every forest passed and every mountain scaled adds to its stature, to the swiftness of its advance, and to the glory of its vision.

The teaching of Jesus concerning the ministry of the austere has greatly changed the popular estimate of the value of many of the experiences through which men pass. Sorrow, pain, and death were formerly regarded as enemies, and only enemies, and they are still so regarded where the full force of His message is either not welcomed or not understood. The common opinion in many quarters, even to this day, is that suffering is either a hideous mistake in the universe, an awful nightmare, or a cruel mockery. Paul, using language as men used it in his time, spoke of death as an enemy. That he was speaking popularly, rather than technically, is evident because he also said that the sting of death - that which made it dreaded - is sin. Jesus, however, justified the method by which men are perfected; and His teaching harmonizes with what may be learned by a reverent scrutiny of the nature of things. The more carefully "the Cosmic process" is studied, the clearer it becomes that events are so ordered that, sooner or later, everything helps toward richer and better conditions. A tidal wave or a pestilence may seem to be inexplicable, but even pestilence teaches men habits of thrift and cleanliness, and tidal waves warn them of their points of danger.

What has made the average of human life so much longer than it was formerly? That very mysterious pestilence has turned attention toward its causes, and thus the race has been made cleaner, purer, more fit to endure. Why do men live in houses with scientific plumbing, fresh air, and have well-cooked food? Because that fierce teacher, pestilence, has taught them that any other course means weakness and death. Whom nature loveth she chasteneth is a truth as clearly written in human history as "Whom the Lord loveth He chasteneth" is written in the Bible. The true attitude toward the austere, for a philosophic as for a Christian mind, is one of complacency. Every severity is intended for benefit. By wars the enormity of war is made evident. By disease the necessity for observation of the laws of health is emphasized. Even death, in the order of things, at last is a blessing, for one generation must give place to another, or the evils that Malthus feared would be quickly reached. Moreover death, in its proper time, is only nature's way of giving the soul its freedom. Hindrances in its path do not indicate the presence of an enemy but of a friend who discovers the only sure way of securing its finest development. The cultivation of the philosophic and Christian temper, which are practically the same, would make this a happier world. We could endure trials with more courage if we would but remember that they are as necessary to our growth as the cutting of a diamond is necessary to the revelation of the treasury of light which it holds.

The heights of character are slowly reached, and, usually, only by the ministry of the austere; but once they are reached the horizon expands, and the soul finds in the clearer light peace if not joy.

This course of reasoning does not make the mistake of regarding sin as less than dreadful. Every sin has hidden in its heart a blessing; but sin as such is never a blessing. It may be necessary for Providence to allow a spirit to sink again into animalism in order that it may be taught its danger, and made to realize that only through struggle can its goal be reached - but the animalism in itself is never beneficent.

When we say that the process by which a man rises may be justified, we do not mean that all his choices are justifiable. The process of his growth provides for his fall, if he will learn in no other way, but it does not necessitate his fall; that is ever because of his own choice. A spirit may choose to return to the slime from which it has emerged. That choice is sin, but it can never be made without the protests of conscience which will not be silenced, and it is by those protests that a man is impelled upward again, and never by the sin in itself. No one was ever helped by his sin, but millions, when they have sinned, have found that the misery was greater than the joy, and this perpetual connection of sin and suffering is the blessed fact. Sin is never anything but hideous. The more unique the genius the more awful and inexcusable his fall. Even out of their sins men do rise, but that is because there sounds in the deeps of the soul a voice which becomes more pathetic in its warning and entreaty, the more it is disregarded. Those who desire to justify sin say that it is the cause of the rising. It may be the occasion, but it is never the cause. The occasion includes the time, place, environment, - but the cause is the impelling force; and sin never impels toward virtue. Satan has not yet turned evangelist.

Because in the past the soul has risen, one need not be unduly optimistic to presume that, in spite of opposition, it will meet no enemies which it will not conquer, and find no heights which it will not be able to scale. Prophecy is the art of reading history forward. The spirit having come thus far, it is not possible to believe that it can ever permanently revert to the conditions from which it has emerged; neither can we believe that it will fail of reaching that development of which its every power and faculty is so distinct a prophecy.

No light has ever yet penetrated far into the mystery of human suffering, sorrow, and sin. Why they need to be at all, has been often asked, but no one has furnished a reply which satisfies many people. With the old insistent and pathetic earnestness millions are still "knocking at nature's door" and asking wherefore they were born. Hosts of others are looking out on desolation and grief, thinking of the tears which have fallen and the sobs which are sure to sound in the future, and asking with eager and pleading intensity, why such things need be.

Out of the heavens above, or out of the earth beneath, no clear answer has come.

As we wonder and study, still deeper grows the mystery. Three courses are open to those who are sensitive to the hard, sad facts of the human condition. One is to say that all things in their essence are just as they seem; that sorrow, sin, death none can escape, that they are evils, and that a world in which they exist is the worst of possible worlds, and that there is neither God nor good anywhere. Then let us eat and drink, for to-morrow we die, and the quicker the end the sweeter the doom.

Another way is simply to confess ignorance. Out of the darkness no voice has come. The veil over the statue of the god of the future has never been lifted, and inquiry concerning such subjects is folly. To this I reply agnosticism is consistent, but it is not wise. Because it cannot explain all things it turns from the clues which may yet lead out of the labyrinth.

The other course, and the wiser, is to use all the light that has yet been given and from what is known to draw rational conclusions concerning what has not yet been fully revealed. Deep in the heart of things is a beneficent and universal law. In accordance with that law hindrances are made to minister to the soul's growth, the opposition of enemies is transmuted into strength, and moral evil resisted becomes a means of spiritual expansion and enlightenment.

THE RE-AWAKENING

I, Galahad, saw the Grail,
The Holy Grail, descend upon the Shrine:
I saw the fiery face as of a child
That smote itself into the bread, and went;
And hither am I come; and never yet
Hath what my sister taught me first to see,
This Holy Thing, fail'd from my side, nor come
Cover'd, but moving with me night and day,
Fainter by day, but always in the night....

     *   *   *   *   *

And in the strength of this I rode,
Shattering all evil customs everywhere,
And past thro' Pagan realms, and made them mine,
And clash'd with Pagan hordes, and bore them down,
And broke thro' all, and in the strength of this
Come victor.

- The Holy Grail. Tennyson.

VI

THE RE-AWAKENING

As despondency and a feeling of failure comes to every soul with the realization of its mistakes and sins, so there will some time come to all a period of Re-awakening. This statement is the expression of a hope which is cherished in the face of much opposing evidence. Nevertheless, that this hope is cherished by so many persons of all classes is a credit to humanity. It is difficult to believe that in the end an infinitely wise and good God will fail of the achievement of His purpose in regard to a single one of His creatures.

The saddest fact in the ascent of the soul is sin. However it may be accounted for, it cannot be evaded, but must be honestly and resolutely faced. Sin is the deliberate choice to return to animalism, for a longer or shorter time, by a being who realizes that he is in a moral order, that he is free, and who has heard the far-off call of a spiritual destiny. It is the choice, by a spirit, of the condition from which it ought to have forever escaped. Imperfection and ignorance are not, in themselves, blameworthy and should never be classified as sins. Weakness always palliates a wrong choice. An evil condition is a misfortune; it does not justify condemnation. Sin always implies a voluntary act. That all men have sinned is a contention not without abundant justification. The better the man the more intensely he is humiliated by the consciousness of moral failure.

After long-continued discipline, after much progress has been made, the soul again and again chooses evil; and, after it ought to have moved far on its upward career, it is found to be a bond-slave of tendencies which should have been forever left behind. This is the solemn fact which faces every student of human life. It is not a doctrine of an effete theology but a continuous human experience. The consciousness of moral failure is terrible and universal. This consciousness requires neither definition nor illustration. Experience is a sufficient witness. Who has been able exhaustively to delineate the soul's humiliation? AEschylus and Sophocles, Shakespeare and Goethe, Shelley, Tennyson, and Browning have but skimmed the surface of the great tragedy of human life. Hamlet, Lear, Macbeth, Faust, and Wilhelm Meister, Beatrice Cenci, the sad, sad story of Guinevere, and the awful shadows of the Ring and the Book - how luridly realistic are all these studies of the downfall of souls and the desolation of character! If they had expressed all there is of life it would be only a long, repulsive tragedy; but happily there is another side. To that brighter phase of the growth of the soul we turn in this chapter.

What is the difference between the awakening of the soul and its re-awakening? Are they two experiences? or different phases of the same experience? The awakening is nearly simultaneous with the dawn of consciousness. It is the adjustment of the soul to its environment - the realization of its self-consciousness as free, as in a moral order, and as possessing mysterious affinities with truth and right. This realization is followed by a period of growth, during which many hindrances are overcome, and in which the ministries of environment, both kindly and austere, help to free it from its limitations and to promote its advance along the spiritual pathway. But while the soul dimly hears voices from above it has not yet, altogether, escaped from the influence of animalism. It dwells in a body whose desires clamor to be gratified. It is like a bird trying to rise into the air when it has not yet acquired the use of its wings. Malign influences are still about it, and earthly attractions are ever drawing it downward. It falls many times. I do not mean that it is compelled to fall, but that, as a matter of fact, its lapses are frequent and discouraging. In the midst of this painful movement upward, there sometime comes to the soul a realization of a presence of which it has scarcely dreamed before. It begins to understand that it is never alone, that its struggle is never hopeless because God and the universe, equally with itself, are concerned for its progress. It is humiliated by its failures, but it has learned that, however many times it may fail and however bitter its disappointment, in the end it must be victorious because neither principalities nor powers, neither things on the earth nor beyond the earth, can forever resist God. Thus hope is born, and he who one moment cries, Who shall deliver from this body of death? the next moment with exultation exclaims, I thank God through Jesus Christ, our Lord.

The light which shines into the soul from Jesus Christ is the revelation of the cooeeperation of the Deity, and of the forces of the universe, with every man who is moving upward. The realization that, however deep the darkness, humiliating the moral failure, constant and imperious the solicitations of animalism, "the nature of things" and the everlasting love are on the side of the soul is its re-awakening.

It now not only knows that it is free, in a moral order, and that voices from a far-off goal are calling it, but also that those who are with it are more than those who can be against it. Thus hope, confidence, power to resist, and faith even in the midst of failure dawn, and will never be permanently eclipsed. The re-awakening of the soul is now complete.

This experience is traditionally called conversion. It is usually associated with an appropriation of the teaching of Jesus Christ, and inevitably follows an appreciation of His words and His work. But all the revelations of the Christ have not been through the historic Jesus. In every land, and in every age, souls have come to this new consciousness. It was said of Isaiah that he saw the Lord; and of Melchizedek that he was the priest of the most high God. The former was a Hebrew, but the latter was not in what was to be the chosen line of succession. The assurance that they are never alone has found many in what has seemed impenetrable darkness, and they have risen and moved upward. Instances of this kind are not limited to Christian lands, although they are most common where the Christian revelation is known. I cannot doubt that those who have not had this vision on the earth will have it some time and somewhere. The Divine power and purpose to save, and to save to the utter-most, are revealed with perfect clearness in the teachings of Jesus Christ. Nothing could be more explicit than His message that God loves all men, and that it is His will that all should repent and come to the knowledge of the truth.

This stage of advance may be called the crisis in the ascent of the soul. Before this it has moved slowly and with faltering steps. Henceforth it will move more confidently and swiftly. But that does not mean that it will find that hindrances are all removed, or that no unseen hand will draw it downward. Some of the bitterest hours are to follow - days and, possibly, longer periods of spiritual obscuration; darkness like that of Jesus in which He cried, "My God, my God, why hast Thou forsaken me." Who can explain the appalling humiliation of a man when, as if a star had fallen from heaven, he sinks into awful and inexplicable selfishness or sensuality? It is not necessary that we explain, but we should remember that the goodness of God has so ordered things that even disgrace may lead to stronger faith, clearer vision, and tenderer sympathy.

Austere ministries are still needed; only fire will consume the dross. The re-awakening of a soul is not its perfecting; but it is its realization that the process of perfecting must go on, and will go on, if need be along a pathway of shame and agony, until all that attracts to the earth and sensuality has disappeared, and the spirit, like a bird released, rises toward the heavens.

The law that whatsoever a man soweth that shall he reap will never be transcended, and if an enlightened spirit ever chooses to sink once more into the slime it may do so; but it will at the same time be taught with terrible intensity the moral bearing of the physical law that what falls from the loftiest height will sink to the deepest depth.

At last the soul realizes that it is in the hands of a sympathetic, holy, and loving Person, a Being who cannot be defeated, and who, in His own time and way, will accomplish His own purposes. That vision of God is the re-awakening, an inevitable and glorious reality in spiritual progress.

What are the causes of this re-awakening? The causes are many and can be stated only in a general way. Moreover, spiritual experiences are individual, and the answer which would apply to one might not to another.

The shock which attends some terrible moral failure, not infrequently, is the proximate cause of the re-awakening of the soul. There is a deep psychological truth in the old phrase, "conviction of sin." Men are thus convicted. Some act of appalling wrong-doing reveals to them the depths of their hearts and forces them in their extremity to look upward. Hawthorne, in his story, "The Scarlet Letter," has depicted the agony of a soul, in the consciousness of its guilt, finding no peace until it dared to do right and to trust God. In the "Marble Faun," in the character of Donatello, the same author has furnished an illustration of one who was startled into a consciousness of manhood and responsibility by his crime. It is the revelation of a soul to itself, not of God to the soul. In Donatello we see a soul awakened to self-consciousness and responsibility, but in "The Scarlet Letter" we have the example of a man inspired to do his duty by the revelation of God. Adoniram Judson was brought to himself by hearing the groans of a dying man in a room adjoining his own in a New England hotel. Luther was forced to serious thought by a flash of lightning which blinded and came near killing him. Pascal was returning to his home at midnight when his carriage halted on the brink of a precipice, and the narrowness of his escape aroused him to a realization of his dependence upon God. The sense of mortality, and the wonder as to what the consequences of wrong-doing in "the dim unknown" may be, have been potent forces in the re-awakening of souls.

Still others have been given new and gracious visions of "the beauty of holiness." They have seen the excellence of virtue, and in its light have learned to hate the causes of their humiliation, and to press forward with courage and hope.

Speculations concerning the causes of this spiritual change are easy, but they are of little value. Observation has never yet collected facts enough to adequately account for the phenomena. Probably the most complete and satisfactory answer that was ever given to such questions was that of Jesus when He was treating of this very subject: "The wind bloweth where it listeth, thou hearest the sound thereof, but canst not tell whence it cometh, and whither it goeth."

The mystery of the soul's re-awakening has never been fathomed. Sometimes there has been flashed upon conscience, apparently without a cause, a deep and awful sense of guilt. Whence did it come? What caused it? Calamities many times sweep through a life as a tornado sweeps over a field of wheat, and when they have passed there is more than an appreciation of loss; there is a vision of the soul's unworthiness and humiliation. Again death comes exceedingly near, and, in a single hour, the solemnities of eternity become vivid, and the soul sees itself in the light of God. And again, the essential glory of goodness is so vividly manifest that the soul instinctively rises out of its sin, and presses upward, as a man wakens from a hideous nightmare. The more such phenomena are studied, the more distinct and significant do they appear and the more impossible becomes the effort to explain them. They may be verified, but they can never be explained. They are the results of the action of the Spirit of God on the spirit of man. Is this answer rejected as fanciful or superstitious? Then some of the most brilliant and significant events in the history of humanity are inexplicable.

What caused the revolution in the character of Augustine by

which the sensualist became a saint? Was it the study of Plato? or the prayers of Monica? or the preaching of Ambrose? We know not; rather let us say it was the Spirit of God. Who can define the process by which Wilberforce was changed from the pet of fashionable society to one of the heroes in the world's great crusade against injustice and oppression? Such inquiries are more easily started than settled. I repeat, the only rational and convincing word that was ever spoken on this subject is that of Jesus. The Spirit of God, whose ministry is as still as the sunlight, as mysterious as the wind, and as potent as gravitation, was the One to whom He pointed.

How has this epoch in the ascent of the soul been treated in literature? I refer with frequency to the literary treatment of spiritual subjects because poets, dramatists, and writers of fiction, more than any other class of authors, have studied the soul in its depths, in its inspirations, and in the process by which it rises and presses toward its goal.

The illustrations of this subject in the Scriptures are almost idyllic in their simplicity and beauty. There is more than flippancy in the remark that Adam's fall was a fall upward. The statement is literally true. The fall was no fiction, but a condition of enlightenment and growth. The exit from Eden was the beginning of the long, hard climb toward the City of God.

The very moment when Isaiah saw Uzziah, the king, stricken with leprosy, he saw the Lord.

The classical delineation of a soul attaining the higher knowledge is that of the prodigal son, who, when he came to himself, saw clearly that his father was waiting to welcome him.

The "Idylls of the King" are a kind of "Pilgrim's Progress." In various ways they trace, and with matchless music rehearse, the growth of souls and their victories over spiritual enemies. One of the most pathetic stories ever told is that of the beautiful

Queen Guinevere, who by shame and agony learned that "we needs must love the highest when we see it;" and who never appreciated the great love in which she was enfolded until Arthur, "moving ghost-like to his doom," had gone to fight his last great battle in the west.

The world owes George MacDonald gratitude it will never repay; - such spiritual souls are never paid in the coin of this world. In "Robert Falconer," he taught his time with a lucidity and sweetness that none but Tennyson and Browning have equaled, and that not even they have surpassed, that a "loving worm within its clod were lovelier than a loveless God upon his Throne," and in "Thomas Wingfold" he has traced with epic fidelity the growth of a soul from moral insensibility to manly strength and vision. The description of the process by which Wingfold is brought to see that he, a teacher in the church, is a fraud and a hypocrite, and by which he is then lifted up and made worthy of his vocation as a minister of the glorious Gospel of the blessed God is a wonderful piece of spiritual delineation.

With Guinevere the external humiliation was an essential stage in her soul's development; but with Wingfold there was no public disgrace, - only the not less poignant shame of a man who, looking into his own heart, finds nothing but selfishness and duplicity. His condition was a matter between himself, his friend, and his God; but none the less the humiliation was the means by which his soul's eyes were opened and his heart fired with a passion for reality.

One result of the soul's re-awakening is the realization that it has relations to God and that they are at once the nearest, the most vital, and the most enduring of all its relations. Before, it had felt the call of duty and had recognized that it had affinities with truth and right; but now it has come into the consciousness of sonship. God is not distant and unrelated, but near and personally helpful. In a very real sense He is Father. He is interested in the welfare of His children; and His will has now become the law of their lives. The first awakening is to the consciousness of a moral order and of freedom; the second awakening is to the consciousness of God and of a near and vital relation with Him. The path of progress is still full of obstacles; there are still attractions for the senses in animalism and solicitations from something malign outside; but never again will the soul be without the realization that it is in the hands of a compassionate, as well as a just, God. I am inclined to think that the elder Calvinists were right in their contention that when the soul has once come to this saving knowledge of God it can never again "fall from grace," or from the consciousness of its relation to the One mighty to save. This does not mean that there may not be repeated and awful moral lapses. The soul's realization of God does not imply that it has become perfected. It has taken a long step in its ascent; it is now conscious of its destiny, and of the power which is working in its behalf; but far away stretch the spiritual heights and, before they can be reached, many a cliff must be scaled and many a glacier passed; and few reach those altitudes without many a savage fall, and without frequent hours of weariness, doubt, and despair. The sufferings and the chastisements of those who have come to this altitude often increase as the vision becomes clearer.

The difference between the former condition and the present is this: in the former there was growth toward God without the conscious choice of God; but in the latter the soul sees and chooses for itself that toward which it has, heretofore, been impelled by the "cosmic process."

That is a solemn and glad moment when, in the midst of the confusion, the soul hears faint and far the call of its destiny; but the one in which it realizes that it is related to God, and chooses His will for its law, is far more glad and solemn. That consciousness may be obscured, but never again will it utterly fail. The soul that knows that it came from God, and is moving toward God, never can lose that knowledge, nor long cease to feel the power of that divine attraction.

A practical question at this stage of our inquiry concerns the relation of one soul to another. May those who have realized this experience help others to attain to it so that the process may be hastened and made easier? Must those who have been enlightened wait for those who are dear to them to be awfully humiliated by sin, or terribly crushed by sorrow, before the light can fall upon their pathway? Is there no way by which a soul may be brought to the knowledge of God except by bitter trials?

One individual may help another to acquire other knowledge, - must it make an exception of things spiritual? That cannot be. What one has learned, in part at least, it may communicate to another, and the constant and growing passion with those who know God is to tell others of Him. All plans of education should include the communication of the highest knowledge. He who seeks the physical or mental development of his boy and cares not to crown his work by helping him to a realization that he is a child of God, and a subject of His love, has sadly misconceived the privilege of education. All curricula should move toward this consciousness as their consummation and culmination. Geology, biology, physiology, the languages, philosophy, the science of society should be so studied as to lead directly to Him in whom all live and move and have their being. The home, the school, the church should be organized so as to obviate, in great measure, the necessity of learning the deepest truths in the school of suffering.

No holier privilege is given to one human soul than that of whispering its secret into the ears of another who has not yet attained the wisdom which comes only by living.

God be merciful to the parent who is anxious about the mental culture of his child and never tells him of the deeper possibilities of his life, or never repeats to him the messages which he has heard in silent and lonely hours. The growth of a soul in the knowledge of God may be measured by the intensity of its desire to help other souls to the same knowledge.

What will the re-awakened soul do? It will be as individual and distinctive in its action as before. The divine life in the souls of men manifests itself in ways as various and numerous as solar energy is manifested in nature. Variety in unity is the law of the spirit. Every person will be led to do those things, to hold those beliefs, and to minister in the ways for which he has been prepared.

The experience of one can never be made the model for another, and the message which the Spirit speaks in the ears of one may never be spoken in the ears of another. Uniformity is neither to be expected nor to be desired. The soul which realizes that it belongs to God will choose to live for Him, and in its own way will forever move toward Him. Henceforward His will will be its law. This is all we know and all we need to know.

THE PLACE OF JESUS CHRIST

I say, the acknowledgment of God in Christ
Accepted by thy reason, solves for thee
All questions in the earth and out of it,
And has so far advanced thee to be wise.

- A Death in the Desert. Browning.

'Tis the weakness in strength that I cry for! my flesh that I seek
In the God-head! I seek and I find it. O Saul, it shall be
A Face like my face that receives thee; a Man like to me,
Thou shalt love and be loved by, for ever: a Hand like this hand
Shall throw open the gates of new life to thee! See the Christ stand!

- Saul. Browning.

VII

THE PLACE OF JESUS CHRIST

In the ascent of the soul do light and power come to its assistance from outside and from above? Is evolution alone a sufficient guarantee that it will some time reach its goal? These are not so much questions of theory as of fact, and as such will be treated in this chapter.

Light and power have come to the race in its struggles upward from one source as from no other. In history one figure appears colossal and unique. Whether we classify Jesus Christ with men, or regard Him as a special divine manifestation is of little consequence in our inquiry. If He is the consummate flower of the evolutionary process, then, because of some unexplained influence, that process reached a degree of perfection in Him that it has reached in no other. If it pleased God in a single instance to hasten the process, the result is not less inspiring and illuminating than it would have been if the divine purpose had been directly and instantly accomplished. The teachers and leaders have ever been helpers of their fellow-men. In evolution, as in the race of life, some always move more swiftly than others; and those who are far in advance may, if they choose, become the servants of those who move more slowly. One Being has appeared in the midst of the ages who is so far superior to all others that He may be regarded as the revelation of the soul's true goal, but who is, at the same time, so unlike others as to convince many, at least, that He is also the revelation in humanity of a higher power which is cooperating with the soul in its ascent.

In this chapter no attempt will be made to meet the various questions that the formal theologians have raised. I cannot feel that such subjects as "satisfaction," "expiation," "plan of salvation" are of any practical importance, and I leave them to those who care for them. In the meantime let us ask, What aid does the soul need in its passage through its life on the earth? It needs light and power. We do not meditate long on the soul's advance without realizing that it has been constantly reinforced from outside itself. This phase of our subject will be considered in the chapter on "The Inseparable Companion."

It may, I think, be said that what the soul needs more than anything else is light, and that all necessary light has been furnished. Jesus said, "I am the Light of the World." That statement is literally true. There may be room for perplexity as to the credibility of parts of the New Testament, and as to what is called the miraculous element in history. There is also room for difference of opinion as to the nature of the person of Jesus, and as to His supernatural mission; but few would deny that, if they could feel sure that He was actually from above, they would accept His message because it contains all the ethical and spiritual knowledge that men need in their earthly lives.

A single assumption is made at the beginning of our study. It is as follows: What satisfies our minds and hearts, in their hours of deepest need and brightest illumination, should always be accepted as true until it is proven to be false.

The profoundest subjects of thought and life are illuminated by the ministry and the teaching of Jesus Christ. The last word concerning these subjects has not yet been spoken. Even our Bible is but a collection of scattered rays of the true light. What vaster revelations may come to men in future ages no one can predict. As growth goes on, the soul will be fitted to receive messages which it could not now understand; but all that men need to know in their present stage of development is clearly revealed in the teaching, and the example, of the Man of Nazareth and Calvary. He is the brightest light on the deepest and darkest problems.

Let us try to understand and define the place of Jesus Christ in the ascent of the soul.

Jesus Christ has given the world a rational and satisfying doctrine of God. Other teachers have tried to answer the inquiry, Does God exist? Jesus treated that question as an astronomer treats the sun. No sane scientist would fill his pages with speculations as to the reality of the sun. It moves and shines in the heavens; beginning with that fact, the astronomer asks concerning the function which the sun performs in the solar system and in the universe.

Jesus discarded speculation and found the key to the doctrine of God in the family, the simplest and most elemental of human institutions. There may be wide differences concerning the nature of government, the sanctions of law, etc., but there is no room for debate concerning the meaning of the parental relation. It interprets itself. Tell a child that a man is his father, and he can be told no more. The name interprets the relation. In earlier times the vastness of the creation was but dimly appreciated, and then the idea of God was equally contracted. Jesus taught that the Deity, whether the conception of Him was small or large, was to be interpreted in terms of father-hood. What an ideal father is to his family God is to the race and to the universe. That meant one thing when the father was little more than the protector of a tribe; it means something greater, but not essentially different now. The conception of the universe is one of the most revolutionary that ever entered the human mind. The conception of a tribe is larger than that of a family; of a nation larger than that of a tribe; of the race larger than that of the nation; but the conception of the universe, with its myriads of worlds and possible multiplicity of races, is the amazing contribution which science has made to the thought of to-day. While the conception of the Deity has been enlarged the principle of interpretation remains unchanged. Are we thinking of Jehovah the God of Israel? He is the Father of the tribe. Has our idea expanded so as to include all the nations? God is the Father not of a limited number but of all that dwell upon the earth. Has the horizon been lifted to take in heavenly heights? Are we now thinking of immensities, eternities, and the cosmic process? The teaching of Jesus is not transcended; we still continue to interpret in terms of fatherhood, and say all time, all space, all men, all purposes and processes in the infinities and eternities are in the hands of the Father. But when we have ascended to such a height what does the word Father mean? Exactly the same in essence that it meant in the humblest of Judean households among which Jesus moved. The father there was the one who made the home, sustained it, defended it, watched over it by day and by night; in exactly the same way the followers of Jesus think of the Spirit who pervades all things. He creates, He cares for, He defends, He provides, He loves, He causes all processes to work for blessing to the intelligent beings who are His children.

Jesus in a peculiar way identified himself with the Deity. That does not mean that all the divine omnipotence and glory were in that Man of Nazareth, but it does mean that all of the Deity that could be expressed in terms of humanity were visible in Him, so that those who saw Jesus saw God as far as He could be manifested in the flesh. Beyond that veil were abysses and heights of being which could not be expressed in human terms; but in all the spaces we may dare to believe that there is nothing essentially different from what was revealed in that unique Man. A bay makes a curve in the Atlantic seaboard; its shallow waters are all from the deeps of the sea. Tides that move along all the seas, and forces which reach to the stars, fill that basin among the hills. The bay is the ocean, but not all of it; for if we were to sail around the earth we should find the same body of water reaching out to vaster spaces.

Even so the person of Jesus included all of God that humanity can contain, but Bethlehem and Jerusalem, Gethsemane and Calvary were to the Deity as some land-locked harbor to the immensities of the universe. In Him love reached to enemies, to the outcast, to those who had been called refuse and rubbish, to men of all classes in all the ages, to lepers, beggars, criminals, lunatics, harlots, thieves, little children; those who appreciated and those who hated alike were all included in the infinite purpose of blessing.

Those who have seen the love of Jesus, and its ministries, have seen the Father; but beyond the love of Galilee and Calvary reach depths of love which even the cross is powerless to express. Divine sympathy and divine affection bind all men in a universal family; this we know, and this is all we know.

That teaching is so simple that a child can understand it; so profound that no philosopher has ever transcended it; and so satisfying that neither child nor philosopher would have it changed either as to its simplicity or its fullness.

Jesus furnishes the light which the soul needs on the nature of man. Wonderfully has Holman Hunt elaborated this truth in his picture "The Light of the World." The ideal humanity never had more beautiful expression than in that great sermon in color. The poise of the figure of Jesus indicates strength and self-control; the thorns on the brow tell their story of sorrow and pain; the hand at the door shows that one man at least is mindful of the welfare of His brother; the radiance on the face and the inspiration in the eyes are the outshining of the goodness which dwells within; while the light from the whole person, which reaches far into the gloom, shows that the more nearly perfect the being the more beneficent and beautiful his influence must be. Is Jesus Christ the brightness of the Father's glory? He reveals also the beauty and helpfulness, the love and the service of the ideal man. He is the pattern of our common humanity. Are we in the midst of a process of evolution? And is the man that is to be still far in the distance? When he shall walk this earth he will be the spiritual reproduction of Jesus, changed only to meet the requirements of other times and new conditions.

The revelation of the ideal humanity was hardly less revolutionary than that of the enlarged universe. Formerly men were regarded as things, commodities to be bought and sold, creatures without souls, objects to be used. But Jesus taught that all men are children of God; therefore that they have the very life of God; therefore that they are created for His eternity, and will forever approach His perfection. This vision of the perfected race has been at work changing national boundaries, destroying hoary institutions, undermining thrones, and making a new world. A glance shows the revolutionary quality of His teaching. Slavery was the curse of every land. With force on the one side and weakness on the other oppression was inevitable. Jesus taught that even weakness may be divine, and lo! from every civilized land slavery has already gone, and from the world it is fast disappearing.

According to the orthodox economic doctrine, supply and demand was the law that should govern the relation between employer and employee. The largest profit and the smallest wages was the watchword. As the teaching of Jesus has penetrated further into the dealings of man with man employers are beginning to realize that labor has to do with human beings; that manhood is enduring and that conditions are ephemeral; and that whosoever oppresses his brother, even in the name of economic law, at last will have to reckon with the Almighty. Thus a new and more beneficent social order is slowly but surely emerging.

The doctrine of the survival of the fittest is, even now, applied to men where the teaching of Jesus that Providence has made a way for the survival of the unfit is unknown or ignored. In all lands the revelation in Jesus of the ideal manhood, and of the destiny toward which all men are moving is changing and glorifying human society. He is the one whom "the low-browed beggar," and the criminal with a vicious heredity, are some time to approach. Is it difficult to select the one phrase of all human utterances which has exerted the largest influence in ameliorating the human condition? Would it not be, -

"Inasmuch as ye did it unto one of the least of these, ye did it unto Me." The identification of humanity with Deity, the revelation of the divine in the human, the solemn truth that no one can injure or neglect his brother without, at the same time, violating all that is sacred and holy in the universe is the culminating point in the revelation of man to himself. In the light which Jesus sheds on humanity all men appear in their enduring rather than their transitory relations.

The life and teaching of Jesus make the awful and insoluble mystery of suffering endurable. He satisfies no curiosity on this subject. Why suffering is permitted He does not tell us. He never allowed himself to be diverted from His one purpose, which was not to solve problems but to improve conditions. If any one approaches the New Testament expecting to find an answer to his speculative questions he will be disappointed; but if he asks, How may I so use the conditions in which I am placed that they will minister to my spiritual purification and power? he will receive a definite and satisfying reply. Why need sorrow, suffering, sin, and death invade the fair realm into which man has been born? Other teachers seek to answer this question but Jesus is silent. How may sorrow, suffering, and even moral evil be made ministers of an upward movement? On this subject Jesus speaks with a tone of authority. Among the world's teachers He was the first to declare that while austere experiences are not good in themselves they may, uniformly, become means of moral and spiritual progress. The sweet may always be found in the bitter. Sorrow may always be made a blessing. Tears never need be wasted. Struggle always adds to strength; and sympathy is multiplied when one bears the grief and carries the burden of another.

Do not brood over what you are called to endure, but seek for the secret of spiritual help which is hidden within, and you will find that on every grief and every pain you may rise, as on stepping-stones, to higher things.

Jesus was the supreme optimist. Those who study life and history in the light which shines from Him see that no human being walks with aimless feet. They do not think of men as unrelated units, but as bound by love to one another, and as living under the eye and in the strength of God. In that light sorrow and pain may be justified, even though in themselves they are hateful. The poison which destroys life, if rightly used, will save life.

Apart from God and His purpose of love, nothing is more to be dreaded than pain; but in His hands pain becomes the servant and not the master of men.

I can think of nothing more dreary than the study of human life and history apart from the interpretations put upon them by Jesus. Then one generation seems to follow another, and the long procession, even though the character of those composing it steadily improves, always ends at the same goal, - the grave. Millions live and die like the beasts that perish. They aspire, struggle, and are determined to rise, but just when they are fitted to endure, and to enter upon ampler spheres of service, the curtain falls on the tragedy, the stage scenery is changed, a new company of players takes their places, and the farce, for it is a farce as well as a tragedy, goes on from century to century, and there is no meaning in anything. If that were the true interpretation of life, on earth's loftiest mountain there might well be raised a temple in honor of death; and around it all the races of men be invited to join in the chorus, "Happy is the next one who dies!"

But a better interpretation of human life's mystery has been given. Jesus looked over its apparent desolation and confusion and poured upon it divine light. He taught that it is not the Father's will that even one should perish. Men are not being ground in an infinite mill, but they are being refined and purified by the only processes which will develop in them both strength and beauty. Out of confusion harmony will come, and out of the battle of the elements peace will dawn at last.

To those who know that pain and sorrow are ministers of strength and sympathy, that by them narrow horizons are widened and deserts made to blossom, human life does not seem so confused and terrible as it has sometimes been pictured. Jesus makes evident the upward movement of the race, and shows, let me repeat, that it is "under the eye and in the strength of God." He was made perfect through suffering. The thorns on His brow tell their own pathetic story. The passion vine above His head, and beneath His feet, indicate that even His sufferings are not without a purpose of blessing, and therefore are fully justified.

And now we approach the saddest of all the dark experiences through which the soul passes, - the mystery of sin. Of its enormity I have already spoken; but what about its origin, its uses, and its continuance? The question of its origin Jesus does not even mention. It is not recognized as having any uses. It may be made an occasion of good, but it is never ordained in order that good may come. Hardly any other subject occupies so large a place in the teachings of Jesus. It was said of Him, "His name shall be called Jesus, for He shall save His people from their sins;" and of Him Paul wrote, "God commendeth His love toward us in that when we were yet sinners Christ died for us."

The terrible blight of moral evil, whatever its genesis, cannot be explained away. Jesus passed by all other questions and devoted the largest part of His ministry, as a teacher, to showing how the soul may escape from the power, and be delivered from the bondage, of sin. This is the practical problem. As one surveys the race the imperative inquiry concerns deliverance. What light does Jesus shed upon this mystery? He shows that sin is an incident in the ascent of the soul, and not an end; that it is hateful and unnatural; and that all the strength and goodness of God are pledged to its removal. The soul will be allowed to be in bondage only so long as is necessary for its complete emancipation. Moral evil is tolerated at all not because it is a good in itself, but in order that the soul may learn that its safety and strength are to be found only in conformity to the will of God.

Jesus reveals the way of escape and thus confers upon the race the greatest of possible blessings. This he does by the revelation of the Fatherhood of God, which is not only compassionate but also holy. Because God is the Father of all souls, when any one ceases to do evil and begins to do well, or in other words repents, he finds a welcome and help waiting for him. And Jesus clearly indicates, also, that in the constitution of the soul, and in the inexorableness of moral law, there is a deep remedial agency which is ever active, giving no individual rest until it finds it in God. The tragedy of the cross was preeminently a revelation. The cross is the manifestation, in terms of human life, of the passion of the universe and of God. There must be suffering in all who are good, until sin disappears.

The cross is the revelation of the Eternal God in sacrifice for the redemption of souls in bondage to selfishness and animalism. Jesus taught that sin is to be abolished. By means of the revelations of holiness, the sacrifices of love, the remedial agency in the universe, and by His own new life the forces of evil are to be broken, and the soul allowed to enter into its freedom as a child of God. This is not a subject for definition and dogmatism. The greatest things cannot be defined, but they may be appropriated. The light, the air, gravitation and all elemental forces transcend definition. The love of God revealed on the cross is too holy and too transcendent for "scheme and plan." It may be accepted in a spirit of worship, but it can be comprehended no more than the process by which rain and soil are transmuted into nourishment, and light into physical strength and beauty. The cross is the pledge of the redemption of the soul through the love and power of God; and beyond that we have no knowledge except that wherever that cross has been lifted up men have been drawn unto truth and virtue, love and brotherhood.

More than poetry and sentiment has found expression in a popular hymn which thrills with a power which has been verified again and again in human history:

"In the cross of Christ I glory,
Towering o'er the wrecks of time
All the light of sacred story
Gathers round its head sublime."

Jesus has furnished no clew to the origin of moral evil, but He has given to the hope that it is to be overcome in the individual, the race, and the universe, the testimony of His teaching and the emphasis of His death.

Which is the greater mystery, life or death? A satisfying answer is impossible, since we cannot think of one without thinking of its opposite. What is life? Whence is it? Why is it? Such are some of the questions which arise and elicit no response when one meditates upon the mystery of living. What is death? What purpose does it serve? Is it an end or a beginning? Such are some of the inquiries which cannot be escaped when one, for even a few moments, looks, as all some time must look, on the still and peaceful face of one who has ceased to breathe. Who shall answer our questions? Of all who have attempted to fathom these depths One alone has brought a message which is satisfying both to the minds and hearts of those who think. Does any light from Jesus penetrate the mystery of death? What others have groped after he has declared. He taught that the universe is like a house of many rooms, and that dying is but passing from one room to another. In His own experience He illustrated His teachings. He ministered to His disciples; He communed with those whom He loved until their hearts burned within them. Then He disappeared and has been seen no more. But why did He appear at all after death? Was it not to confirm the message of the Transfiguration that those who seem to die only change the mode of their existence, and continue their companionships and ministries even after they have laid aside their bodies?

In the passage in the Gospel of Matthew, which may be called the parable of the judgment, Jesus taught that the moral order is not changed by the transition from bodily to disembodied existence. The thoughts which men think, and the actions which they perform, affect the substance of the soul. Evil works misery and virtue leads to happiness beyond the grave as well as here. Seed sown on the earth may grow to its harvest in the ages that lie beyond.

This is all the light on this subject that we need now. Death removes no one beyond the watch and care of the infinite love. In the home of the Heavenly Father His children pass from place to place, as He calls. Jesus appeared to those who loved Him, and was recognized by them, and that indicates that, whatever the changes of the future, the spiritual body will be recognized by all who love.

The moral order is universal, and no change will touch the everlasting distinctions between right and wrong, or diminish the obligation to choose the right and refuse the wrong.

These are some of the lessons which are impressed upon us as we meditate upon the life and teachings of Jesus and their relation to the ascent of the soul.

He is the light of all souls. Into the darkness His glory has been extending and expanding from His own time until now. If we may judge the future from the past, it is easy to believe that this radiance will not fail from among men until all realize that life and death, time and eternity, humanity and history, are beset behind and before by the Divine Fatherhood; that the goal of the race is the fullness of Christ; that the severest experiences sometimes achieve the best results; that sin will not forever darken the history of humanity; that death is a passage not an abyss; an opening not a closing; a beginning not an ending; and that beyond stretch opportunities of limitless life and immortal growth.

THE INSEPARABLE COMPANION

The prayers I make will then be sweet indeed,
If Thou the Spirit give by which I pray:
My unassisted heart is barren clay,
Which of its native self can nothing feed:
Of good and pious works Thou art the seed,
Which quickens only where Thou say'st it may
Unless Thou show to us Thine own true way,
No man can find it: Father! Thou must lead.
Do Thou, then, breathe those thoughts into my mind
By which such virtue may in me be bred
That in Thy holy footsteps I may tread;
The fetters of my tongue do Thou unbind,
That I may have the power to sing of Thee,
And sound Thy praises everlastingly.

- Sonnet from Michael Angelo. Wordsworth.

VIII

THE INSEPARABLE COMPANION

As the soul moves along its upward pathway it gradually becomes conscious of many inspiring truths. Among the most delightful and helpful of these is the fact that it is never alone, but is one of a great company all pressing toward the same goal and all passing through substantially the same experiences. In the midst of these companionships, which are variable, and of these experiences which can seldom be predicted, it slowly becomes aware that there is one companionship which is constant, beneficent, and singularly illuminating. The realization of this fellowship is intensely individual. Of it others may speak, but concerning it they can give little information. The full consciousness is always a personal one. Having once enjoyed communion with the Over-soul it is difficult to imagine that any are ever without this supreme spiritual privilege. Sometimes the sense of spiritual cooeperation is so vivid and continuous, so compassionate and helpful, as to be almost startling - in those moments when it seems to beset us behind and before. The process by which a soul becomes conscious that it is forever attended by a companion, whose one object seems to be to help it toward the spiritual heights, will repay the most careful examination. To that delightful and difficult study we will now turn.

Before it has advanced far on its pathway the soul becomes painfully aware of the dangers by which it is surrounded and of the obstacles which it must overcome. The road before it seems to be infested with enemies. Its defeats are frequent and humiliating. It learns much by experience; but the more it learns the clearer it seems to discern the difficulties which it must meet. In the midst of the confusion and failure it slowly becomes aware that warning voices are speaking, and that they are loudest when moral peril is near. This is one of those simple facts which may be verified by every thoughtful man, but which no thoughtful man would ever dream of trying to explain. So simple and elemental is this truth that it may best be enforced by commonplace illustrations, and by something like a personal appeal.

A very distinguished man was one day walking with a friend along a street in Edinburgh, when they came to one of the numerous wynds which lead from the main thoroughfare into the midst of huge and gloomy buildings. There the man stopped and asked to be excused while he entered the wynd. Returning, after a moment, he explained his act by saying that, in his young manhood, he had been tempted to do something which would have wrecked his life. Just as he came to the place that he had visited there sounded in his ears such a vivid warning as made it morally impossible for him to proceed on his course of wrong-doing. He felt sure that that voice was from above, for his whole nature, until that instant, seemed to have been set on what would have led to moral ruin.

Another person testified that he was once on the verge of doing what would have brought him undying disgrace when, as if she had been drawn out of the air, his mother stood before him, looking reproachfully at him. Thus the fascination of temptation was broken by what he always believed to have been a veritable spiritual presence.

Another experience is perfectly attested. A man in a distinguished position did wrong, and was in peril of still greater wrong when something, he could not have explained what, not only warned him but kept warning him and following him so that he could not escape. If he closed his eyes his danger became more vivid; if he stopped his ears voices of reproach found their way in. He loved his wrong and would move toward it, but then invisible hands seemed to hold him back until the time of danger was past, and he was confirmed in right ways. Such experiences are too numerous and varied to be doubted. No facts are better attested. It may be said that they are only the usual warnings of conscience. Be it so. Then what is conscience? The factors in the problem are not materially changed, for the phenomena of conscience are as remarkable, constant, and verifiable as light and heat. Most men who have recorded their experiences, and who have observed with care the workings of their own faculties, have been conscious of being attended by some invisible presence warning them against evil. The explanation of this phenomenon may be left for later consideration.

Closely allied to warnings against moral danger, which are so vivid as sometimes to be almost audible, are the evidences of what may be called spiritual protection. The idea of guardian angels and tutelary deities arose naturally and inevitably. Many who have been astonishingly delivered from spiritual peril have been able to find no other explanation of their escape. Those who receive the confidences of their fellow-men have little difficulty in believing such a story as was once confided to me. An able and prominent man who had, resolutely as he thought, turned from a course of conduct which threatened disaster, found himself drawn toward the evil from which he supposed that he had been forever delivered. The attraction seemed to be resistless. Again and again he was on the verge of falling when the fall would have been ruin. Then something made it morally impossible for him to enter upon the path which he had determined to follow. The means used to dissuade him were various. Sometimes a friend would call, then a duty would intervene, then some obligation would press until, to use his own way of phrasing it, - "it seemed as if some unseen person who could read my thoughts and desires was walking by my side and, as fast as I was in danger of yielding to evil, ordering events so as to prevent me from doing what I wanted to do."

Few men who are trying to live on spiritual levels would hesitate to acknowledge that they have been the subjects of similar protection. The peculiar feature about it all is that the agents used are so often entirely unconscious of the influence which they are exerting. An unseen hand seems to be guiding our moves on the chess-board of life, so as to check us every time that we are inclined to play falsely. I do not mean that all are persuaded toward virtue, but I do mean that enough are protected from moral evil and spiritual peril to justify the belief that such ministries are around all; and that those who choose to do wrong do so in the face of spiritual appeals which, if they would but give them heed, would make resistance of evil easy and successful. If any one who reads these words doubts my conclusions, let him study his own life, with a little care, and learn for himself whether there are not many hours in which he is almost persuaded to accept the ancient doctrine of guardian angels.

This phase of the spiritual experience is rendered still more vivid when we remember that the souls of men are perpetually dissatisfied with present attainments, and ever eager in their efforts to explore the unseen. The history of human thought, if it could be written, would show that the mind has never been satisfied with what it has possessed, and that each new glimpse of truth has stimulated still more ardent inquiry. The more it is pondered the more impressive this fact becomes. The soul seems to have had just before it, in all the stages of its development, a spiritual forerunner opening a way into larger and fairer realms. This consciousness is not akin to a passion for wealth. A man with enormous riches often ceases to acquire, and devotes himself to the enjoyment of what he possesses; but who ever heard of a thoughtful man who felt that he might cease investigating and devote himself to the pleasures of knowledge? Such instances there may have been, but they are not numerous and have never been recorded.

Of course there are many, who in no true sense can be called seekers after truth, who do not trouble themselves with questions about the Unseen. They chew the cud of custom with all the placidity of good-natured oxen. They do not live, - they simply exist. It is possible for any man to shut his eyes to the light, but that does not banish the light. It envelops him, and pours its splendors around him, regardless of his wilful blindness. Millions are so engrossed with selfishness, or animalism, that they catch the accents of no spiritual message, but those appeals are never hushed. The deafness of the multitudes who will not hear does not prove that no voices are calling.

In some way men have been kept dissatisfied with their ignorance and persistent in their search for truth. I make no distinction between sacred and secular here because all truth is sacred. Scientist and theologian alike have to do with reality. Whether we examine the tracks of an extinct animal on ancient rocks, or bow our heads in prayer, we are facing a real world which is steadily enlarging. For centuries men have sought the causes of things; they have been made to feel that they ought to do right, and then have been inspired with a passion to discover the right. This is very wonderful. The being who has almost limitless powers of physical enjoyment, whose senses are exquisitely fitted for pleasure, is not satisfied with pleasure, but, in obedience to unseen attractions, ever seeks for higher things. Whence does this eagerness come? Is it from man himself? Then our problem is great indeed, for, at one and the same time, something within himself impels him upward, and another something drags him downward. But the point for special consideration now is that the soul is never satisfied with anything but truth, that the history of thought is the record of the search for truth, that every new discovery has acted as a stimulus to still more ardent exploration, and that the search is always for elemental realities, the causes of phenomena, for "things as they are." The promise of Jesus was fulfilled long before it was spoken. Some one, in all the ages, has been leading into truth and showing things to come; and the process was never more evident than after all these years of intellectual and spiritual progress. I say some one has led. By that I mean a personal spirit, unseen, but ever present; for how could he whose home is in the mire be supposed, steadily and unwaveringly, to reach toward the skies unless there was some attraction in the skies? The only attraction for one spirit is another spirit. This age-long, unwavering passion for truth and progress, the wisest of men have believed to have been inspired by Providence or God or by guardian angels - which after all are only other ways of stating the doctrine of Jesus concerning the Holy Spirit.

Another phase of this subject is the power, which has seemed to come from outside the soul, to sustain and help those who have been called to endure bitter and long-continued sorrow and pain. Those who feel themselves to be weak as water under the stress of severe trial, almost without previous suggestion, assume the proportions of heroes. They endure and suffer with patience what would crush those who are only physically brave and strong. A woman who seemed to have few resources in herself, suddenly lost four children. In speaking of it, she very simply but forcefully, said: "I could never have endured it myself." She believed that her fragility had been reinforced by one stronger than herself. Exceptional physical courage will account for deeds of amazing heroism like that displayed at the sinking of the Merrimac in the harbor of Santiago. Some persons are thus gifted by nature, as others have a poetic temperament. But exhibitions of physical valor, stimulated by the consciousness of world-wide applause, are very different from the patience with which weak persons accept heavy burdens without a murmur, and carry them apparently without assistance, sustained only by the consciousness of being right.

How shall we explain the singular devotion of Monica to Augustine? By mother-love? But mother-love might have been content with the greatness of her son, and his regard for her. She bore on her heart "the salvation of his soul," and would not cease in her quest for his spiritual welfare. A profligate father, the degraded ideals which justified vice, distances which seemed to be almost world-wide, did not daunt her. Without haste and without rest she sought to bring her gifted son to his Saviour. He had fame, and at least all the wealth that he needed, but Monica never faltered in her prayers, or in her service, until her son bowed before the cross, albeit for years she carried a heavy heart.

The age of martyrdom has passed but not the age in which men of vision and strength have to serve their fellow-men with neither pecuniary compensation nor expressed approval. And yet the number is steadily increasing who quietly undertake herculean tasks for their fellow-men, knowing that they will be neither appreciated nor understood, but, instead, will have to suffer social ostracism, which is sometimes quite as hard to endure as physical martyrdom. When a strong and earnest man undertakes a service in which he must be misunderstood, and seldom if ever applauded, when he chooses suffering with joy in order that he may serve others, when he is willing to accept discomfort, social hunger, physical pain, and without complaint continue in such a path, although opportunities of worldly emolument and honor make their appeals to him, it is difficult to explain the phenomena by simply saying that he is finding strength in some hitherto unknown chamber of his own personality. It would be easy to make a list of illustrations, long and pathetic, of those who have patiently endured tribulation, who have accepted heavy burdens and carried them without flinching that others might be relieved, who have had physical deformity, depression of mind, and pain of body, and yet who have never faltered as to their duty even when the way was dark. The world's noblest heroes are to be found among those who suffer but still endure and aspire in the night and silence, clinging to duty when no one understands, and much less approves. Such heroisms need explanation, and they have it in the inspiration and the regeneration which are mediated by the Inseparable Spiritual Companion.

Phenomena like those of which I have thus far been speaking have been observed in every age and every land. Some like Socrates have felt themselves warned against evil courses; others like Augustine have been protected from moral and spiritual death; others like Sakya-Muni have been led to give up wealth and power for truth and service; others, who could draw upon no hidden source of strength, have been sustained in the midst of trials which have seemed heavy enough to crush; and, most wonderful of all, in spite of all vices and crimes, all darkness and ignorance, all bondage to ignoble ideals and slavery to commercialism and pleasure, the race of man has never been content with things as they have been. As the moon draws the tides by unseen attractions, so by unseen attractions the souls of men have been made dissatisfied, and drawn toward truth and beauty, love and holiness; and this desire for some better country has never been absent. The passage from Egypt to the promised land is the eternal parable of humanity, which is always getting out of some Egypt, with its slavery and tyranny, and pressing toward some intellectual and spiritual Canaan. This is one of the most marvelous facts in the history of our race - its discontent with things as they are, its faith in something better, and the perfect confidence with which it embarks on unknown seas in its search for ampler and fairer worlds.

The history of the past is the record of the weak receiving strength, of the wicked being made uncomfortable in their wickedness, of limited and provincial creatures reaching out to broad and high horizons, of weakness, suffering, agony, willingly endured in the confidence that relief and blessing will come at last, though far off, to all.

Moreover, there is no indication of any cessation of such phenomena. In these days, when we say that no man should be asked to affirm anything which he cannot verify, voices of warning and entreaty are vivid, the consciousness of protection is distinct, support in trial is frequent, and the evidence that some force, or some person, is steadily leading humanity toward truth and righteousness is as convincing and constant as ever.

What shall be said of these facts which are so numerous and so evident as to make an effort at classification and explanation imperative?

Amory H. Bradford

Four answers to this inquiry are possible. Is the old doctrine of Guardian Angels true? Possibly we may be, individually, under the care of spiritual beings who are appointed for that service. That conviction often prevails, although so far as I have observed, not usually in association with perfect sanity. A man of noble bearing and grave and solemn manner who was talking about using the telephone for trans-Atlantic communication, once declared that all men living now are under the leadership of those who have gone, and that the great of other times are continuing their work through those now on earth. He added: "I am confident of my success for I am the representative in these days of Sir Isaac Newton." Subsequent events proved that Sir Isaac Newton must have lost most of his common sense since his departure from the earth, or he would have chosen a more rational representative.

This theory in no way solves the problem before us, but rather complicates it, because it does not explain how the relation of souls is adjusted. That there may be some truth in this speculation may be freely granted. One text at least appears to give it a little confirmation: "Are not their angels ministering spirits sent forth to minister to such as shall be the heirs of salvation." That seems to teach that some who have never dwelt in earthly bodies are the appointed ministers of those who live on the earth.

Many other persons dismiss this subject by saying that all souls, like all objects in nature and events in history, are parts of an everlasting and universal process, and that speculation is useless and a weariness to the flesh. That is the easiest way out of the difficulty, but it can be taken only by ignoring the facts. Are all ideas concerning spiritual ministry delusions? Then how shall we account for the imagination which is capable of giving birth to such magnificent dreams? And we may venture to ask also - Who started this movement in which we are all involved? How comes it that in this cosmic loom such a wondrous fabric is being woven, if there is no pattern, and no weaver, and will be no one to enjoy the work when it is finished?

Possibly no one is warned against sin, impelled toward virtue, supported in sorrow, led into larger visions of truth; and, possibly, truth and right are also dreams, and the mind itself a delusion; and, possibly, there is nothing but delusion. Then all study and struggle are useless; let us go to sleep. But, some one else says, perhaps the phenomena of which you speak are, in one sense, realities but caused by reactions of the soul on itself. First it imagines that some spiritual leadership is desirable, and then it concludes that that leadership is discernible. In other words, sorrow, sin, relief, joy, truth, right, are only imaginations born of other imaginations. If any are satisfied with such reasoning the task of enlightening them is hopeless.

There is another explanation of the sublime, ancient, and world-wide facts which are before us. It is the answer of Jesus, which is simple, profound, rational, and satisfying. He told His disciples, when they were grieving that they should see Him no more, that they would always have with them the Spirit of Truth who would convict of sin, show things to come, and lead into all truth. That Spirit in the Scriptures is called by one of the sweetest and dearest names in the languages of men - the Comforter. Some have wrongly imagined that the New Testament teaches that the presence of the Comforter is a new event in human history. Not so. The Spirit of Truth inspired and sustained the Apostles and Martyrs as He had sustained the Patriarchs and Prophets and the same Spirit which is represented as descending upon Jesus at His baptism brooded upon the face of the waters when the earth was without form and void.

Jesus teaches that God, as a Spirit, has never been absent from His creation and never out of touch with the spirits of men. In the beginning He created; later He inspired, supported, taught, comforted; and always and everywhere He is present to sustain, to lead, to comfort, to help, to save, and to bless. How simple, rational, and satisfying is this interpretation of the phenomena of human history!

We study our own spiritual experiences and discover that hen we have been in danger of being contented with moral failure we have been made ashamed and disgusted by it; that when we have been on the verge of yielding to temptation we have been strangely and almost preternaturally protected; that when sorrows have come which would have crushed our unaided strength we have experienced strange peace and have had undreamed-of strength; and that never for a moment have we found rest or peace except as they have come to us in hand with truth and right. A wider study shows us that our experiences are in harmony with the common human experience. All forces and all events, in all ages, have been working for the welfare of individuals, society, the whole world. A steady, unfailing, universal attraction has been drawing the human race away from animalism, error, sorrow, war, separation and division, toward righteousness, truth, love, brotherhood, the life of the Spirit, and the unity and happiness of the children of God.

That attraction is interpreted by Jesus in a simple and beautiful way. He has taught us that the same Being who created the universe, and who has revealed and is revealing Himself in creation, in history, and in the earthly ministry of the Christ, is now, always has been, and always will be in the most intimate, personal, and loving relations with men. He warns them against evil, protects them in danger, comforts them in sorrow, lifts their thoughts and desires toward the true, the beautiful, and the good; and what He is doing for individuals He is also doing for humanity and the universe. This is the culmination of the Christian Revelation. This is to be the consummation and splendor of the Kingdom of God. All the disciples of Jesus are followers of the Spirit of Truth. The Spirit of Truth is the inspiration of all that is vital and enduring in literature, art, government, society; and each individual, and "the whole cosmic process" are being led by Him toward the beatitude of the Children of God.

NURTURE AND CULTURE

O happy house! whose little ones are given
Early to Thee, in faith and prayer, -
To Thee, their Friend, who from the heights of heaven
Guards them with more than mother's care.
O happy house! where little voices
Their glad hosannas love to raise,
And childhood's lisping tongue rejoices
To bring new songs of love and praise.

O happy house! and happy servitude!
Where all alike one Master own;
Where daily duty, in Thy strength pursued,
Is never hard nor toilsome known;
Where each one serves Thee, meek and lowly,
Whatever thine appointments be,
Till common tasks seem great and holy,
When they are done as unto Thee.

- *O Happy House.* Karl J.P. Spitta.

IX

NURTURE AND CULTURE

In the ascent of the soul two forces are ever at work: one is internal and the other external. The internal is that which promotes growth; it is resident within the soul, and, while it may be modified by conditions, it is in no sense dependent on them. But environment is a potent factor in all progress. Life necessitates growth, but environment determines the end toward which it will move. Environment in large part is composed of the circumstances into which we are born, of the spiritual companionship from which none can escape, and of the training which is provided by parents and friends. So much of the environment as is furnished by others we will call nurture, and those influences and instruments of advancement which the soul chooses for itself we will call culture. This discrimination is not entirely accurate, but it is sufficiently so for our present purpose. It at least indicates the lines along which our thought will move. According to this definition nurture has to do with that period of our existence when we are not able wisely to make choices for ourselves. It is for those persons who are in infancy and early youth, and also for those whose normal development has been thwarted or hindered. The influences of the home, and of the church so far as they are related to its younger members, are in the line of nurture rather than of culture.

Culture, on the other hand, is something which a responsible being seeks for himself, to the end that his power may be increased and his faculties have harmonious development.

The soul grows according to its innate tendencies; it is also subject to attractions from without. All souls are bound together; and all, whether they wish or not, vitally and permanently affect those by whom they are surrounded. Hence nurture and culture alike are both conscious and unconscious.

The growth of the soul is largely affected by the nurture which it receives. This is usually provided for it by parents, or by those who take the places of the parents; and, where possible, their unwearying efforts should be to remove all obstacles from the pathway of their children, to surround them with a pure and helpful environment, and to provide them with such training as will make their progress inevitable and easy. The importance of wholesome domestic influences cannot be exaggerated. Their part in the formation of character is greater than that of all others, because they touch the powers and faculties of the child during those years in which it is most plastic. Neither the school nor the university can ever entirely counteract the effect of the home. The whole period of childhood is one in which the soul is under tutelage, and in which more is done for it by others than by itself. It can no more select its own environment than it could have chosen its parents, or the time and place of its birth. For a few years it is utterly dependent. The question as to how its growth may most wisely be promoted is, therefore, one of surpassing importance.

The object of nurture is to provide an unhindered path along which the soul may move, to bring into full and free exercise all the powers which it possesses, and to secure for them development and harmony. To insure for each individual soul in the struggle of life a fair opportunity to be itself is the end of nurture. Emerson has said that at birth every child is loaded with bias, and that the purpose of culture is to remove all impediment and bias, and to secure a balance among the faculties so as to leave nothing but pure power. The same may be said as to the object of nurture. Since impediment and bias are never a part of the essence of the soul, the statement that the aim of nurture is to furnish a full and free opportunity for each individual to secure a normal development is, practically, identical with what Emerson has said of culture.

What are the agencies which have most to do with promoting the ascent of the soul? The first is atmosphere. In a bright, clear, sunshiny atmosphere the body attains its most healthful growth. So with the soul. Atmosphere is one of those intangible things that every one understands and no one can easily define. It is composed of a thousand different elements. The atmosphere of a household is the spirit by which it is pervaded. Are all reverent, earnest, cheerful, optimistic? Do love and mutual helpfulness prevail? Do the members of the family live as if God were a near and blessed reality, and right and duty were more sacred than life? Then there will be an atmosphere of hopefulness, devotion, service, reverence, pure religion, which will affect all as sunlight and air, unconsciously but evidently, grow into the beauty and fruitfulness of meadows and gardens. The rare spirituality, the urbane manner, the exquisite regard for others, the dignity and deference which are found in some persons have no explanation except that they have been absorbed from the households in which their early lives were passed. Nurture is chiefly a matter of mental and spiritual atmosphere. Attraction is always stronger than compulsion. A child born into conditions in which love prevails, where truth, duty, honor, are reverenced, and where all dwelling together seek the highest things, will need neither instruction in morals nor motives in religion. It will naturally turn toward truth and righteousness. It will revere virtue and worship God as inevitably and spontaneously as it breathes. We are all influenced more by the words which we hear and the examples which we see than by the lessons given us to learn, by the spirit of a man, or an institution, rather than by rules. Persons show the conditions in which they have been reared by their choice of words, their bearing, the subjects of their conversation, by their mental and spiritual attitude. Reverence is seldom found except in an atmosphere of reverence, and sincerity grows among those who are sincere. It is a moral necessity that some men should be earnest and enthusiastic, and impossible for their neighbors to be other than cringing and mean. The largest element in environment is atmosphere, and in the development of character environment is quite as potent as heredity. Indeed, in the sphere of the spirit, as in that of the body, heredity is always modified by environment. The chief factor in nurture, therefore, is atmosphere. If that is healthful, growth will be toward beauty and strength; if that is malarial, no antiseptic force but the grace of God will be able to counteract its influence.

Next to atmosphere as an element in nurture I place ideals. For these children are usually dependent on their elders. They reverence what they are taught to revere. Ideals are placed before them by example and by precept. Children grow like those whose deeds attract them, and they seek those ideals toward which they are most wisely directed. Laws are never as potent in the formation of character as examples. Men are made brave by the sight of bravery, and honorable by contact with those who will swear to their own hurt and change not. There is deep philosophy in the saying that the songs of a people influence their institutions and history more than legal enactments, for songs are usually of bravery, of love, of victory. They create ideals; they excite enthusiasm. The Marseillaise and The Watch on the Rhine send thrills through the blood of those who hear them because in the most vivid way they suggest patriotism and heroism. A good man inspires goodness. Philanthropy makes others philanthropic. One courageous act sometimes makes heroes of a hundred common men. If a father would have his son physically brave, and he is a wise parent, he will not waste time in urging him to undertake some forlorn hope, but he will read to him the story of the Greeks at Thermopylae, of Marshal Ney at Waterloo, of Nathan Hale and his holy martyrdom, of Nelson at Trafalgar. If he would have that son a helper and servant of his fellow-men he will tell him the story of Pastor Fliedner and his work at Kaiserwerth, of Florence Nightingale at the Crimea, of Wilberforce and Buxton, Whittier and Garrison in their efforts to awaken their fellow-men to the enormity of human slavery. The strongest force for making a young man brave and generous, honorable and Christian, is the example of a father possessing such qualities. Men are usually like their ideals, and their ideals in large part are created by the examples of those who are most admired and loved.

But example is not all. Training also does much. Conduct is but the expression of thought. If one can determine what shall be the subject of another's thinking, he will have gone a long way toward fixing his character. This is a fact which deserves more attention than it has yet received in plans for the education of the people. Parents have no holier privilege than that of directing the thought of their children. By their own conversation, by the friends whom they invite to their homes, by the books which are given a place on their tables, by the amusements to which they take their families, they determine for them the channels in which their minds shall run. As a man thinketh in his heart so is he. Boys usually dwell upon the same subjects as their fathers, unless the fathers by skilful conversation are able to hide the subjects to which they give most time. Children usually admire what their parents admire, and shun what they shun. The organic unity of the household is a large factor in individual and social progress. Both by direct effort, and by the indirect operation of example, it furnishes subjects for the youthful mind. The personality, whose seat is in the will, is never determined, but it is very largely influenced both by the example of those who are admired and by the thoughts which they suggest.

Environment in large part is composed of atmosphere, example, and ideals. All these are provided for the growing child by others. He has little or no voice in saying what they shall be. And environment has more to do with the progress of the soul toward full and free self-expression even than what is called education. Education is more by atmosphere, example, and mental suggestion than by teachers and text-books. When we speak of nurture we usually think of the period of discipline in school and church; but we often make the mistake of not taking into account the fact that the most effective training is seldom that which comes directly from teachers. It is rather that which is derived indirectly from the atmosphere, example, and ideals by which the child is surrounded in his home. If I could determine those for a child I should dread very little any malign force in the shape of an incompetent teacher. Schools, in reality, are only for the unfinished work of the homes. They may make the child better than his home, and they may undo the good work which it has done; but, usually, what the home is the child will be some time.

The agencies of nurture, by which a soul is helped on its upward pathway, are atmosphere, example, ideals, and direct training. Of these the least important is the last, although the value of that is self-evident. By the intellectual and spiritual air that we breathe, by the sight of heroic and consecrated service, by the possibilities of noble achievement the best that is in a man or a boy is usually drawn out. Afterward the teacher may take him in hand and, by training, remove the impediment and bias and thus make a balance in the faculties, or take out of his way the obstacles which oppose his progress; but he seldom does very much toward determining the direction in which the child will move. That is decided by others in the years which are most plastic. The soul naturally, and inevitably, grows toward truth and God. How could it be otherwise, since its being is derived from Him? But a part of the mystery of growth is the influence of environment, and early environment is almost altogether composed of the circumstances and influences into which one is born.

The question of nurture, therefore, is of vital importance. What shall one generation do for those which are to come after it? Each soul may hinder or help the growth of countless other souls. The influence of those nearest is always most potent for good or ill. Impediment is increased, and bias exaggerated, by evil example. The effort to rise becomes easy when the way is seen to be full of those whom we love and honor going before us toward the heights, and it is difficult when no familiar face is seen. Nurture is not so much a matter of teacher and text-book, of church and catechism, as of atmosphere, example, and inspiration. It is the effect of the contact of one pure and noble soul upon another; it is something which father, mother, and friends give to the child; it is the result of the spirit in which they impart instruction and of the reverence and consecration which shine from their lives.

The best and only enduring nurture is that of a sweet, serene, optimistic, and thoroughly Christian environment. With that, inherited tendencies toward weakness and evil will go of themselves, - indeed will seem never to have had existence.

But all too soon the time comes in which the soul faces its own responsibility, and realizes that it must choose for itself what its course shall be. It has learned, if it has observed, that there is ever with it an unseen leadership, and it has heard, faint and far, the call of a noble destiny. What shall it now do for itself? Shall it choose simply to exist? Shall it yield to the limitations and solicitations of the body? or, shall it seek to prepare itself by discipline, and the cultivation of right choices, for the goal whose intimations it has heard? Nurture, if it has been wise, has been the forerunner of culture. Atmosphere and example have inspired lofty ideals, but those ideals, if they are to be realized, will require training. Matthew Arnold, quoting Bishop Wilson, has said that culture "is a study of perfection." In other words, it is the means which are used for the perfection of the soul. Shall we choose to leave ourselves to grow like trees in a forest, however they may, or shall we seek those conditions which will make progress sure and swift? Culture is always a matter of choice; and it is vastly more than anything which can be taught in the college or university. The cultured man is he who has learned so to use the forces and conditions of life as to make them minister to his perfection. The one most cultured may come out of a factory, and the man of least culture may be found in a university. Indeed colleges and universities, not infrequently, are haunts of provincialism and of dread of enthusiasm. The object of culture is the perfection of the spirit to the end that all that hinders, or limits, may disappear and only pure power, clear vision, and full self-realization remain. Those whose growth is most evident are ever eager to use all experiences as means of progress. They study books in order that they may better understand what others have thought concerning the mystery of existence; they discipline their minds in order that they may the better serve their fellow-men; they seek fineness of manner and beauty of expression to the end that their utterance of truth may be more persuasive and convincing. Culture and the discipline of life are identical. Consequently, the wise man chooses to put himself where he will best be taught by the events through which he passes, by what he sees, and by what he may learn from others. It matters little who have been the teachers, or what have been the schools, - the real teacher is always life, and the real university is the human experience.

I do not make light of the benefit which may be derived from books and institutions of learning, but I do insist on the recognition of the deeper fact that the lessons which no one can afford to neglect are those which can be taught only by overcoming obstacles. We can learn how to live only in the school of life. The most vital books are always those which tell us what others have done, and of the paths by which they have been led to power. What shall the soul do for itself in order that it may promote its own growth? It must first recognize where the sources of knowledge and strength are to be found, and then put itself where it will feel the touch of the vitality which can come only from other souls. Quickly enough every man reaches the time in which he may determine his own environment. When we are young others choose our circumstances for us, but when we become older we select them for ourselves. That means much. No monarch is mighty enough to compel me to associate with those who will hinder my progress. He only is a slave whose mind and will are in bondage. My body may be with boors but, at the same time, my spirit may be holding companionship with seers and sages. I may be compelled to work in a mine like John the Apostle, but I, too, like him may hear One speaking whose voice is as the sound of many waters, and whose eyes are like a flame of fire. Our real associates are ever our spiritual companions; and

126   Amory H. Bradford

no one can force another to hold fellowship with those who are either intellectually or spiritually uncongenial.

And we also select our own subjects of thought. Who can govern the thinking of another? At the very moment when one, who is stronger, is rejoicing in what seems his supremacy, our thoughts may be ranging through the spaces, and finding companionships among the stars. And we choose our own examples. In youth they were put before us according to the will of others, but later our heroes come to us at our bidding, and no one can shut the gates against them. Whom shall we admire? Let them be men of the spirit, who have sought truth and hated lies, "who have fought their doubts and gathered strength," who would rather suffer wrong than do wrong. The perfection of being is the end of effort, therefore we will read what will best help our growth in vision, in moral earnestness, in spiritual sensibility; therefore our books shall treat of subjects which will ennoble; our amusements shall be pure and clean; and our chief companionships shall be with the prophets and masters, the noble and the good, because by associating with them we shall become like them.

Intellectual acuteness, mastery of faculty, elegance of expression, are something very different from insight into the meaning of life. The cultured man is he who has learned his relations to his fellow-men, who recognizes his obligations toward them; and his relations to the unseen and his duty toward it.

Discipline which will produce such results will ever be sought by the awakened soul. It will be satisfied with nothing less.

The relation of nurture and culture to the ascent of the soul is now evident. Both are the agencies by which all impediment and bias are to be removed, and by which the soul is to come to the realization of pure power. They are the means by which complete self-realization is to be attained; they are the study of perfection. Nurture is what is done for the soul by parents and friends in its plastic years; culture is the means which the soul chooses in order that its growth may be hastened. Nurture is chiefly promoted by lofty examples, noble ideals, - in short, by beneficent environment; but culture is attained by the conscious effort of the individual, by his own choice of healthful environment, worthy example, inspiring companionships, and, perhaps still more, by long and patient study of the facts of our mortal life, of the revelations which have come from the unseen, and of the prophecies of the future which are within the soul. There is a deep and almost terrible significance in the text, "No man liveth to himself." Every person is independent and free and yet is bound to every other. Most delicate and vital of all human relations is that of parent and child. How far one may be responsible for the other may be difficult to decide, but that the one influences the other, inevitably and forever, is beyond question. In many ways the child is what he is made by the parent. Therefore the welfare of the child as a spirit, and not merely as a body, should be a continual study. He who has dared to become a parent can never honorably shirk the duty of nurture. The connection between souls is a great mystery, but the mystery does not lessen the obligation. We are responsible not only for the existence of our children, but equally for their growth. It is the parent's privilege to make sure that they start on the journey of life properly equipped, and with no undue obstacles in their pathway - to make them realize that they are not only his children but also children of God; and that they are to live not only in time but in eternity.

The training of the body is needful, and that of the mind still more so, but that of the spirit is absolutely essential to its welfare. Therefore plans and provisions for nurture first, last, and always should be to the end that the soul may realize that it is from God, and that its goal and glory are union with Him.

And those who realize that they are free, that they are in a moral order, that a noble destiny awaits them, should make everything in thought, in study, in association, in companionship, bend toward the perfection of being, the development of power, and the realization of the life of the spirit. Nurture does much for every man, his parents and friends also do much but, at last, when all mysteries are disclosed and self-revelation is complete, it may be found that each one does quite as much for himself as any one else, or every one else, does for him.

IS DEATH THE END?

It's wiser being good than bad;
It's safer being meek than fierce;
It's fitter being sane than mad.
My own hope is, a sun will pierce
The thickest cloud earth ever stretched;
That after Last, returns the First,
Though a wide compass round be fetched;
That what began best, can't end worst,
Nor what God blessed once, prove accurst.

- *Apparent Failure.* Browning.

X

IS DEATH THE END?

We have been studying the ascent of the soul in the successive stages of its development, from the dawn of consciousness to the measure of progress which our race has now attained. But a dark shadow falls across that history. No one has yet lived who has reached what all have believed to be the fullness of his possible development. At a certain period in physical history what we call death intervenes, and we are left wondering as to whether that is the end of all, or whether the soul persists and continues its advance unhindered by bodily limitations. That death is the end of the body, in its present form, no one doubts; but whether the relations of the soul to the body are so intimate and enduring that what vitally affects one affects the other is a subject concerning which there has been eager and constant inquiry, and but little real knowledge. Job's question, "If a man die shall he live again?" is the common question of humanity. The importance of the subject is attested by the prominence which it has always had in human thought. Philosophers have given it foremost place in their speculations. Science, while seeking to explore every part of the physical universe, never escapes from the fascination of this question. Is the death of the body the end of the spirit? Or, if we have not sufficient material for a positive statement, is there enough to make a strong affirmation of probability? We are facing the deepest mystery which is ever presented to thinking men. Heretofore we have been trying to follow a history clearly marked in the progress of humanity; now we can only balance probabilities. But all that has been learned concerning the nature and development of the spirit of man not only warrants, but compels, the belief that death is not the end of the soul; and that to assert that it is, is to deny the revelations of the universe, and to insist that there is nothing but irony and mockery where there ought to be reason and wisdom. In treating this subject I can but repeat thoughts which have been emphasized again and again; but it is so vital, and so near to the welfare of all, that old arguments become new, and interest in them increases, the more frequently they are emphasized.

On what do we base our faith that the soul exists after death? That it does is clearly the faith not only of religious teachers but of many of the latest and most eminent scientists. Many expounders of evolutionary philosophy unite in telling us that "the cosmic process" having reached man, a spiritual being, can go no further in the physical order; that evolution will never produce a higher being than a spirit, but that the "cosmic" force will still persist and be utilized in the expansion and perfection of spirits.

In treating this subject little attention will be given to the scriptural argument, for there is little if any difference of opinion concerning the teaching of Jesus and that of the writers of the New Testament. They are united and consistent in assuming the persistence of being. That belief underlies all their appeals to the solemn sanctions of the moral law which they derived from the future life. Jesus himself said, "If it were not so, I would have told you;" and nearly, if not quite all the Apostles base their warnings and their invitations on motives which reach beyond the death of the body. The masters of other religions have been equally positive. In some form or other they have asserted the continued existence of the spiritual nature in man.

But we turn, for the moment, from these and consider such evidence as may be derived from the soul itself, and from what is known of its progress.

There is no evidence that when the body dies the soul dies with it. It may not be possible to prove the reverse; all that we know is that the vital functions cease, and that the body decays. No eye ever saw the soul, and no dissection ever discovered the place of its dwelling. Is that ethereal something which we call soul simply the result of the organization of atoms? Or is the body like a house in which a spiritual tenant dwells? At least this may be affirmed: No one has yet been able to prove that the soul and body die together. Then there is no reasonable presumption against the continuance of being. No spirit, so far as we know, has returned to the earth in visible form, and spoken its message; and yet, for aught we know, we may be surrounded every day by spiritual beings, moving unseen along the avenues upon which we walk, and entering without invitation the houses which we inhabit. At this point it is enough simply to grant that presumptions are, perhaps, evenly balanced. If one asks for proof that the spirit persists, the only reply must be a Socratic one - Can you prove that it is vitally connected with the body?

Belief in the existence of the soul after death seems to be an innate belief. It has been ascribed to the influence of the superstition about ghosts; but that superstition is only an unscientific form of the larger faith in the persistence of being. Where did this conviction originate? We think only of such things as have been experienced. No thought is ever entirely original. Even imagination cannot create anything absolutely unlike anything which ever existed. All the fabled beings who, according to the ancient mythology, filled the spaces and waters, were but human creatures adapted to imaginary environments. Faith in the existence of the soul after death could not have originated in the soul itself; to believe that would be to contradict the laws of thought. It seems to have been born with the soul, and yet not to be a part of it.

The common conviction of continuance of being can be explained only on the assumption that it is an innate idea. That this assumption starts, perhaps, quite as many questions as it settles may be granted. Nevertheless, it is the only way in which this fact in mental and spiritual history can be accounted for.

Not only is belief in persistence of being innate, but it is also universal. It has been found in every land, in every time, in every religion. Dr. Matthewson has finely argued that the savage worships a fetish because he is seeking something which does not change[8]. He knows that he dies; he worships that which he thinks does not die. A piece of wood or a stone, at first, seems to him more enduring than a man; therefore he worships the fetish. Gradually his eyes are opened and he realizes that the man is more enduring than the thing. Then the object of his worship is lifted from something material to a spiritual being. The belief in immortality is coterminous with belief in the Deity; the two forms of faith are always found together. The cultured Greek, the mystic Egyptian, the idealistic Indian, the savage who inhabits the forests of Africa, or who formerly dwelt in the forests of America, alike have believed in some land of spirits to which their loved ones have gone and to which they themselves, in turn, will also go. Every age and every time, alike, have borne witness to the strength and vitality of this faith.

[Footnote 8: Distinctive Messages of the Old Religions, p. 9.]

But still more convincing to me than any of the suggestions which have gone before, is the fact that it is irrational to suppose that the soul dies with the body. If that were true, how could we account for the enormous waste in discipline and culture, in education and affection? What is the meaning of the love that binds human beings together, if after a short "three-score-and-ten career" it utterly ceases to be, and being and affection alike go into oblivion? How can our systems of education be justified, if the soul is perfected only to be destroyed? On everything else man spends time, labor, affection in proportion to the possibility of its endurance. He never seeks that which he knows will be taken from him and destroyed as soon as it is perfected. An artist would not spend a lifetime on a picture, or a sculptor in finishing a statue, if he knew that when his work was completed it would be instantly sunk in the depths of the sea. We devote a large part of our lives to education; we cultivate our minds; our affections are disciplined; we spend time, money, labor for years for the culture of our children; can it be that all this preparation is for something which never can be realized? In the midst of the loftiest manifestations of the soul's power the body ceases to be. With indescribable bravery a warrior lays down his life, a fireman rescues a child from a burning building, a life-boatman goes through the surf to a sinking ship, and, at that very moment when he proves himself best fitted to live, death comes and he is seen no more. It cannot be proven that this is not the end, but it is not reasonable to believe that this is the end. If it is, human life is utterly without significance, and he is most to be commended who quickest escapes from its misery and mockery.

Moreover the inequalities of the human condition are strangely prophetic. Much has been made of this argument in the past, - Job and Socrates both felt its force.

The value of it has often been discredited, but without reason. How shall the bitter injustice which is frequently found on the earth be explained? Some have an abundance of wealth, some have literally nothing. Some enjoy the best of health and strength all their days, while others pass their years in suffering and trial. Some are surrounded by families and fairly revel in love and friendship, and others lead lonely lives toward a welcome end. Some are strong and brave, and able to act a part in the drama of life; others are weak, obscure, unknown, and, for aught that they or we can see, might as well have never been. The law of heredity sweeps down from the past and brings a terrible legacy to many who spend all their days in trying to escape from what has been forced upon them. What shall we say concerning those who are born in lust and must live in the midst of the vice of a great city, and who, in turn, give birth to a lustful and vicious brood? Have they had a fair chance? Will their children have? Such questions have puzzled the most earnest thinkers of all time, and there has seemed to be but one explanation. Job seemed to be in darkness, until at last there flashed upon his mind this question, which is also a modified affirmation, "If a man die shall he live again?" If he live again, then it is possible that what seems to be unjust may be righted; and those who have known only suffering and pain during their dwelling in the flesh, may some time enter into the fruition of their discipline in the joy and victory of the endless life. The more this argument is pondered the stronger its force becomes. It carries conviction to all who are deeply sensitive to the common human experience, and who at all understand the misery and the suffering of human existence. One in the fullness of his physical strength may think little about it, but that deformed girl who asked her mother after service one Easter Day, "Mother, is it true that in heaven I shall be as straight as you and father?" is a type of millions of others. Some suffer in body and some in mind; some have a heredity of insanity or vice - they are born with shackles on their faculties. If they ever have a fair chance to grow noble and beautiful, morally and spiritually, it must be after their bodies have been laid aside. It cannot be said that they do not now desire benefit and blessing, but it is evident that it is impossible for their longing to be gratified. The conviction that this is a moral and rational universe compels us to believe that some time and somewhere those who suffer will escape from their pain, that those who are burdened with the evil that has been inherited from past generations will rise above it, and that the soul will be given an unhindered opportunity for growth and advancement. The inequalities in the human condition almost compel us to believe that the death of the body cannot be the end of the spirit.

A little light on this subject comes from the faith of the world's greatest teachers. As there are, now and then, those who see farther than others with the physical eye, so there have been a few teachers who have been rightly called seers, because their eyes have penetrated farther into the mysteries of the universe than have those of their fellow-men. Among the seers of the ages, I think that the two whom all would recognize as being preeminent are Socrates and Jesus - the one the finest flower of the intellectual development of Greece, and the other the consummation of the hopes and visions of the most spiritual people that the world has ever known. Both Socrates and Jesus believed in God, and both have taught the world, with no uncertain sound, of their faith in immortal life. The latter was clearly an axiom with Jesus, for He said to His disciples in effect, "If there had been any question about it I would have told you;" and almost with his last breath Socrates compelled his disciples to think of him as immortal, for he told them that, though his body might be buried anywhere, he defied both friend and foe to catch his soul. Socrates and Jesus represent the belief of the world's greatest seers.

The deep and abiding confidence of the teachers, who increasingly command our admiration as the years go by, is not to be entirely disregarded. We may care little what those tell us who walk by our sides in the dark valleys or on the dusty plains; but there are others who have climbed to the crests of the loftiest mountains, and who have looked into a world of which we have only dreamed. When they come down we listen because we know that they have had visions. Even so it is in our intellectual life. A few men have risen above the common levels of humanity, as the Alps above the plains of Lombardy. They have spoken concerning what they have seen. They have had glimpses of God - the soul of the universe, and of the persistence of individuals in the realm that lies beyond the grave. I might not let my faith be determined by their testimony alone, but when what they say is confirmed by many other voices speaking in the soul, and sounding through the history of the world, it is easy to believe that they have spoken of things which have been revealed to them.

Another confirmation of our conviction of the reality of life after death may be stated as follows: It is not possible for us to think of the heroes and singers of the ages as having less endurance than the words which they have uttered and the deeds which they have performed. Milton's and Shakespeare's bodies have long been dead. The great dramatist has recorded a dire curse on any one who should move his bones. In the chancel of the Church of the Holy Trinity at Stratford-on-Avon those bones are supposed to rest. But the plays that Shakespeare wrote are still the wonder of the world, and the glory of the English race. Is it possible to believe that the man was less enduring than his work? Is it possible to believe that Shakespeare's plays and Milton's epic will exist, perhaps, for a thousand years, while the dramatist himself has utterly ceased to be? You open a neglected drawer of your desk and come suddenly upon a letter written by a friend of half a century ago; the paper is a little soiled, but as firm as ever; the ink is hardly faded; the words are all clearly formed and full of inspiration; and you hold that letter in your hand and ask yourself, "Was the man who penned these lines less enduring than the paper on which he wrote, or than the ink with which he wrote?" Such questions are not arguments, and yet they have the force of arguments. It is not possible in our better moments to feel that the great and good, by whom this world has been lifted to its present condition, have gone entirely into nothingness.

It was said of our Lord, "It was not possible that such a man should be holden of death." And it is not possible for us to believe, in our inmost souls, that those who become a part of our being, whose love is of more value to us than our own lives, whose memory is the dearest treasure that we possess, by some accident, a taint in the food or the water, can utterly pass from existence. If it were possible to believe that, then the most miserable creature on the earth would be man, for he would know of his greatness, and know also that his greatness is a mockery and a sham. In hours of doubt, let us lean hard upon the question, "Is it possible that those with whom we have walked and worked, conversed and communed, and by whom we have been helped and blessed, should forever cease to be, while the houses in which they live, and the tools with which they labor, will endure for generations?"

The soul is full of prophecies. Only as there may be continuance of being can these prophecies have fulfillment. The feeling of dependence, the desires for friendship which are never satisfied, the powers of body and of mind which are capable of a development which they never receive on earth, are prophecies of a life beyond death. Not the least among the reasons for our belief that death is not the end of the soul is the fact that the soul itself is a prophecy of its own immortality.

It is always best to believe the best. This world and human life may be interpreted on the materialistic hypothesis; then matter is all and death is the gloomy *finale* to the tragedy of existence. Or they may be interpreted according to the spiritual hypothesis; then within the body dwells the spirit; then the latter is but a tenant of the former. If the house is destroyed the tenant goes elsewhere. If we interpret the world, and human life, according to the materialistic theory all the beauty and joy of existence on the earth will disappear. We will then live for a little time; and our loves, our disciplines, and our victories alike will be only delusions soon to be mercifully ended by death. Possibly that is true; but, if it is true, then this universe is the embodiment of the most dismal, desolate, and diabolical thought that it is possible for a human being to conceive. On the spiritual hypothesis all experiences are intended for the perfection of the soul. Bodily limitations, physical sufferings, animal solicitations, may all be used so as to promote the development and perfection of the spirit. When the body can do no more the soul will emerge purified and strengthened by contact with that which is physical. It will then move from the narrow quarters in which it has dwelt into some larger and fairer room in the great palace of God. Once more, I confess, we cannot demonstrate the truth of this faith, but it is always best for ourselves and for the world to believe the best. With this faith human life is nobler, and human effort more persistent and enduring than it would be without it. At the end "the finished product" will be larger, and more perfect, if there is something to strive for than if hope is destroyed the moment that aspiration is born. I should be willing to rest my faith in immortality upon this one argument. A rational being should be satisfied only with a rational answer to his questions; a moral being should be satisfied only with a moral solution of his problems. This universe is neither rational nor moral if the soul ceases to be at the death of the body. On the other hand, if the soul passes into another and ampler sphere all the mysteries are explained, and there is meaning even in the darkest passages of human experience. All things work together for good to those who are willing to be led toward the higher things.

These are some of the reasons, with which all thinking persons are familiar, for believing that the soul continues its growth after the body has been laid aside. Evolution has opened a new vista in human thought. There had been vague suggestions of it before, but evolution has done much to confirm faith by its clear and strong testimony. It prophesies the eternal growth of the spirit. These prophecies are harmonious with those of the soul, and with the positive teachings of the Christian revelation. This then is our conclusion: - in the process of time, in accordance with natural law, our bodies will be laid aside, some in one way and some in another, but the soul that has dwelt in these bodies will become free. In ways of which we know not, and of which it would be presumption to speak, its perfecting will be continued. What teachers will take it in hand then is beyond our knowledge; but we are confident that its individual existence will continue, that its perfection will be along moral and spiritual lines, that it will grow forever and forever in intelligence, in love, in the power of rational choice, and into harmony with Him from whom it has come and whose glory will be its perfection. To believe less would be to refuse to listen to the voices which speak within and the voices which speak without, - it would be to believe in an irrational and immoral universe rather than a rational and moral one.

Our souls have a right to be heard, and their prophecies have in them an element of certainty. He who listens to the voices which speak within will never believe that the death of the body is the end of his personal being. The suggestion of a state of existence from which sin, sorrow, and death shall be forever absent, into which there shall enter nothing that maketh a lie, and where sacrificial love is the everlasting light, is the highest and most satisfying ideal for human life that has ever been spoken or imagined; and that which completely satisfies the heart cannot at the same time be repudiated by the intellect.

Let us, therefore, reverently confess that we believe in "the life everlasting."

PRAYERS FOR THE DEAD

Thy voice is on the rolling air;
I hear thee where the waters run;
Thou standest in the rising sun,
And in the setting thou art fair.

What art thou then? I cannot guess;
But tho' I seem in star and flower
To feel thee some diffusive power,
I do not therefore love thee less:

My love involves the love before;
My love is vaster passion now;
Tho' mixed with God and Nature thou,
I seem to love thee more and more.

Far off thou art, but ever nigh;
I have thee still, and I rejoice;
I prosper, circled with thy voice;
I shall not lose thee tho' I die.

- *In Memoriam.* Tennyson.

XI

PRAYERS FOR THE DEAD

The wisest of men have little to guide them when they approach that mysterious realm from which no traveler has ever returned. With humility and the consciousness that we must, at the best, walk in the twilight, I take up one of the most mysterious and fascinating of themes. No one has any right to speak positively on such a subject, and I shall not do so. Those who have the assurance of sight when they write about what lies beyond the grave are both to be envied and to be pitied, - envied because of their confidence, pitied because they may be self-deceived.

Let me make my exact purpose as plain as I can by an illustration. A dear friend, one with whom you have associated for years, enters the silent life. The morning following, as has long been your custom, you offer your prayers to the Heavenly Father, and, as usual, mention that friend by name. Suddenly you stop and say to yourself, "I can no more offer that petition, for my friend is now beyond the need of my poor prayers." Then, suddenly and swiftly, come the questions, Although my friend is called dead is he any less alive than when he was in the body? Will not all that constituted his personality continue to grow in the future as in the past? Does the death of the body do anything more than change the mode of the spirit's existence? And the result is that you say to yourself, "I will continue to pray for my friend, for, if he is alive now, every reason which led to prayers before his death justifies their continuance."

From more than one person I have heard words similar to these which I have put into this hypothetical form; and because of these expressions of sane and sacred experience I am led to ask my readers to follow me in the consideration of a subject which is seldom mentioned, except with incredulity, by most Protestants.

No one who may not appreciate the importance of this subject should be either troubled or heedless. We learn our lessons concerning the profounder mysteries simply by living. No one can be blamed for not appreciating what he is not yet, either intellectually or spiritually, ready to receive. Providence takes good care of us. When we are prepared for the reception of any truth it usually finds us.

This subject has been regarded with suspicion by two classes of thinkers: Protestants who have revolted from the extent to which praying for the dead has been carried in the Roman Catholic Church, and the much smaller number who hold what they delight in affirming is "the true theology," and who have insisted that when men die their state is irrevocably and forever fixed, the good going at once into the perfect bliss of heaven and the wicked into the suffering of hell.

It will be more profitable for us to deal with the positive side of our subject than to attempt to clear away misconceptions and half truths.

What is meant by prayers for the dead? Exactly the same as prayers for those in the body. When the body dies the soul, or the essential man, is not touched by death. The personality is that which thinks, chooses, lives. Your mother is not the form on which your eyes rested, or the arms which encircled you, but the thought, the devotion, the affection concealed, yet revealed, by the body, and which use it for their instrument. In reality we never saw our dearest friends; what we saw was color, form, but never the spirit. That is disclosed through the body, but is not identified with it. Now just as we have prayed for a mother, or a child, or a friend whose physical form is familiar, but whose personality we have seen only in its revelations, so we continue to pray for that loved one which we do not see any more, or any less, after what is called death.

In other words, instead of thinking of any as dead, we think of all as alive, although many of them are in the unseen sphere. Love and sympathy have never been dependent on the body except for expression, and there is no evidence that they ever will be. Sympathy and affection, thought and will, are matters of spirit; and why may not spirit feel for spirit and minister to spirit, when the body is laid aside? Your hands, your feet, your lips did not pray for your child; your spirit prayed for his spirit, and now that his body is laid aside, like a worn-out garment, you may keep on doing just what you did before. This is what is meant by prayers for the dead.

I am well aware that it may seem to some that these statements rest largely on assumptions, but they are not baseless assumptions. One other assumption must be made before we can proceed in our study, and that one is the truthfulness of the Christian teaching that death is not cessation of being, but only the decay of the bodily organism.

How may prayers for the dead be justified? Are they taught as a duty in the Scriptures? The privilege rests not so much on particular exhortations as upon the whole Christian teaching concerning immortality. God is the God of the living. Bishop Pearson in his exposition of the Apostles' Creed has an impressive passage, which I quote: "The communion of saints in the Church of Christ with those who are departed is demonstrated by their communion with the saints alive. For if I have a communion with a saint of God, as such, while he liveth here, I must still have communion with him when he is departed hence; because the foundation of that communion cannot be removed by death. The mystical union between Christ and His Church ... is the true foundation of that communion.... But death, which is nothing else but the separation of the soul from the body, maketh no separation in the mystical union, no breach of the spiritual conjunction, and consequently there must be the same communion, because there remaineth the same foundation."[9]

[Footnote 9: Quoted in Welldon's "Hope of Immortality," page 332.]

Jesus taught that death is but a change of the form of existence. On the Mount of Transfiguration Moses and Elijah appeared alive, and as interested in human affairs. If death is not cessation of being, but only a change in the form of its manifestation, why should we think that human sympathy ends when breathing ceases, and why should we conclude that mutual service may be rendered impossible by "a snake's bite or a falling tile." Tennyson in "In Memoriam" gives the Christian doctrine exquisite expression,

"Eternal form shall still divide
The eternal soul from all beside;
And I shall know him when we meet."

Jesus teaches the reality of immortality He represents those gone from us as not dead but as still living and still interested in human affairs. If His teaching is true, is it not as reasonable to try to serve those of our loved ones who are out of the body as those who are in the body? So far as we can see, the only way in which we can serve them is by prayer, although they may, possibly, minister to us in other ways.

If immortal existence means the possibility of unceasing growth, then every reason which prompts prayer for those who are bodily present remains a motive when they have entered the state which is purely spiritual.

But what efficacy will prayers for the dead have? My answer is two-fold. All the efficacy that prayer ever has. If death is relative only to a single state of existence, and if those whom we call dead are living, and still free agents, then they may still choose good and evil, and they may still grow toward virtue. Choice always implies a possibility of freedom; and freedom is a necessity when there is moral responsibility. If prayer helps any one, why not those who have passed from our sight? Surely we must believe them still to possess the power of choice and, therefore, that of choosing evil as well as good.

You ask why pray at all. My answer is simple and free from all attempts at casuistry: simply because we must. Prayer is not so much a Christian doctrine as a human necessity. It is as natural as breathing. By prayer I mean not only spoken petitions but, equally, the longing and pleading of the soul, either blindly or intelligently, for things which are beyond our reach, and which only a higher Power can provide. Those longings may have formal expression, and they may not. Prayer so far as it is petition is the soul pleading with the Unseen for what it deeply desires. I do not suppose that God needs light from any mortal man, but all men do need many things from Him, and, as naturally as children present their desires to earthly parents, even though they know them to be already favorable, we go with our deeper needs to our Heavenly Father.

Much time has been wasted in trying to formulate a rational basis for prayer. When a child in the smaller family no longer asks his father to accede to his wishes, when he no more pleads with his father for his brother or his sister, then it will be time enough to inquire if, in the larger family which we call humanity, we may do without prayer. Until then let us believe,

"More things are wrought by prayer
Than this world dreams of."

Leaving now the apologetic side of the subject, which is alluring, we observe one evident blessing which always attends praying for the dead. It keeps ever before our minds the thought that they are actually alive. It makes the doctrine of the communion of saints a sacred reality. If I may in this essay be allowed to assume a hortatory tone I will say, if you have been in the habit of praying for your friend, do not give it up simply because he has ceased to breathe. As regularly as ever continue to pray for him, and he will be to you more than a memory. What would have been but an occasional remembrance will then be a daily communion; and what would have been only formal praying to God will be an hour, or a moment, of association with those who will grow nearer and dearer, and not farther and vaguer, with the passing years. The hour of devotion will thus be hallowed, because it will be a holy tryst with absent friends, as well as a time for making our requests known to our Heavenly Father. Who can exaggerate the delight and benefit of such an exercise? What sources of strength are to be found in spiritual association with our beloved! If we are thus helped why should we presume that they may not also, by such sweet hours, be strengthened for their duties? I know this may seem fanciful. I ask no one to follow me who is not ready to do so. I do not speak dogmatically, but with great earnestness, when I say that prayer for our beloved after they are gone is a privilege and a help - I would fain believe both to them and to us.

But it may be objected that the moral state of men is fixed at death, and that nothing that we or they can do can influence it by a hair's breadth. That this has been a popular opinion is true; and it is equally true that many have supposed that all who have had faith on the earth are in bliss; and that all who have been without faith are in misery; and that the beatitude of all the good is equal and alike, and that the misery of all unbelievers is the same.

Such inferences, though held by many for whose scholarship and character I have profound reverence, seem to me to be contrary to Scripture, to the analogies of nature, and to the moral sense. Such a theory is contrary to Christian Scriptures; for the parable of the talents shows that some will have greater and some lesser reward; and the parable of Dives and Lazarus has relation only to Hades, or to the state which in the thought of that time intervened between death and the judgment.

This theory is contrary to the analogies of life on earth. Here change indicates not a finality but a new opportunity. Every crisis of life is an opening into a newer and larger world. Why should we say that what we call death, alone of all the changes through which we pass, leads to that which is unchangeable?

The theory is contrary to the moral sense of all earnest souls. Who does not have to compel himself to believe, and that with difficulty, that death determines forever the fate of all, and that there is neither possibility of progress nor of going backward after the body is laid aside?

Let me quote a noble passage from Bishop Welldon: "But if a variety of destinies in the unseen world, whether of happiness or of suffering, is reserved for mankind, and yet more, if the principle of that world is not inactivity but energy or character or life, it is reasonable to believe that the souls which enter upon the future state with the taint of sin clinging to them, in whatever form or degree, will be slowly cleansed by a disciplinary or purifactory process from whatever it is that, being evil in itself, necessarily obstructs or obscures the vision of God." He continues, "And this is the benediction of human nature, to feel that, as souls upon earth are fortified and elevated by the prayers offered for them in the unseen world, so too by our prayers may the souls which have passed behind the veil be lifted higher and higher into the knowledge and contemplation and fruition of God."[10]

[Footnote 10: The Hope of Immortality, page 337.]

We do not know that death forever determines the condition of the soul. On the other hand, as I grow older, the idea seems to me to be opposed to Scripture, to the analogies of nature and history, to reason, and to the universal moral sense.

If any one should object to prayers for the dead because the privilege and duty seem so distinctively a doctrine of the Roman Catholic Church, my only reply is that we should never ask who are the advocates of any teaching, but, only, is it true? Each branch of the church emphasizes some phase of truth. The Roman Church has given more prominence to prayers for the dead than Protestants, and because of that it will have the gratitude of many honest souls who cannot believe that they are entirely and forever severed from those whom they have loved and still love.

I am well aware that there are many difficult questions concerning this subject which it is impossible for me to answer. Some truths are clearly revealed and of others we have only glimpses. Concerning some we feel more than we know, and feelings which are not selfish are prophetic. What an earnest and inquiring spirit feels must be true is quite as likely to be found true as conclusions which seem to have been reached by a process of faultless logic.

I fully believe that we are justified in praying for those who have departed this life, that the good may grow better, that the clouds which obscure the vision of the unbelieving may be removed, that all taints of animalism may be washed away; and that we should pray even for the wicked, that the disciplinary processes through which they are passing may some time and somehow lead them to submit their wills to the love and truth of God. We may pray for our loved ones, not simply by way of asking something for them, but in order that there may be a meeting place, - a time for communion and fellowship between those here and those beyond the veil. That meeting place must be found in our common approach to God.

Does this teaching seem mystical and fanciful? What if it does? It is in line with the human heart's deepest desires, and with the soul's immortal aspirations. What they most earnestly affirm in their hours of deepest need, and highest illumination, cannot be altogether without foundation in reason and in the Scriptures.

The unity of life cannot be too strongly emphasized. Life is one. It is all under the eye and in the strength of God. It has to do with spirit; death, if there is any such thing, has to do with matter. Spirits always grow because they always live. The universe is not composed of two hemispheres, in the upper one of which are to be gathered all the good and in the lower all the evil. It is saner and better to believe that the universe is a sphere in which, in their own places, are all the spirits of men, some beautiful with the holiness of God; some only beginning to rise toward Him, like seed that has broken the soil and begun to move toward the light; and still others like seed whose possibilities are all hidden, but which are not destroyed and which some day also will hear the divine call, feel the touch of God's light, and begin to move toward Him.

We live in the midst of mystery. In the future we shall probably find that our best attempts at rational answers to many questions have gone wide of the mark. The most that any of us can do is to be true to ourselves, and to respond to every call from above. In the midst of the gloom of mortal existence it is safe to follow our hearts.

We long to commune with those who have gone, to help them and to be helped by them. This longing is natural and rational. That it is not without reason is proved by the example of our Master, who, after His death, is represented as ministering to those whom He loved, and who, we are told, ever liveth to make intercession for us.

What our hearts desire, what harmonizes with reason, what is confirmed by the revelations and example of our divine Teacher, will persuade none far from the path which leads to light and felicity.

Those whom men call dead, it is best to believe, have but entered upon another phase of the eternal life of the spirit.

The Roman Church has an act or service called "The Culture of the Dead." It means the "practice of the presence" of those who, though gone from us, in spirit are with us. The Creed has an article which reads, "I believe in the communion of saints." The Christian year has one day called "All Saints' Day." We shall not be far from the traditions of the church when we pray for our beloved, whether they be in the body or out of the body.

Those who would realize the beatitude of this privilege should remember the truth in this stanza from "In Memoriam:"

"How pure at heart and sound in head,
With what Divine affections bold,
Should be the man whose thought would hold
An hour's communion with the dead."

THE GOAL

But Thee, but Thee, O Sovereign Seer of time,
But Thee, O poet's Poet, Wisdom's Tongue,
But Thee, O man's best Man, O love's best Love,
O perfect life in perfect labor writ,
O all men's Comrade, Servant, King, or Priest, -
What *if* or *yet*, what mole, what flaw, what lapse,
What least defect or shadow of defect,
What rumor, tattled by an enemy,
Of inference loose, what lack of grace
Even in torture's grasp, or sleep's, or death's, -
Oh, what amiss may I forgive in Thee,
Jesus, good Paragon, thou Crystal Christ?

- *The Crystal.* Sidney Lanier.

XII

THE GOAL

If the cosmic process in the physical sphere culminated with the appearance of man, and if, since that culmination, its movement has been toward the perfection of the soul, it is fit and proper that this book should end with a study of the goal toward which the human spirit is pressing. Is it possible for us, with our limitations, to have an adequate conception of the man that is to be "when the times are ripe" and the "crowning race" walks this earth of ours? - or, if not this earth, at least, dwells in the spiritual city? The fascination of this subject has been widely recognized. The answer must be secured from many sources. Only in imagination can we follow the lines along which the spirit will move in the far-off ages, and yet our conclusions will not be wholly imaginative, for the direction in which those lines are tending is clearly perceived. Under the circumstances, therefore, imagination may not be an untrustworthy guide. We are now to deal with prophecies, some of them easy and some of them difficult to read. But reading prophecies is not prophesying. I shall not prophesy, but rather endeavor to understand and to interpret a few of the many voices which have spoken, and are speaking, on this subject.

The soul is itself a prediction of what it is to be. It utters a various language.

The growth of intelligence is prophetic. Savage tribes suggest the original condition of primitive man. The pigmies in Africa afford hints of Adam and Eve, Cain and Abel. From such as they, and from lower types still, the race has slowly and painfully risen. In them a certain rude intelligence appears. They have cunning rather than reason. They are half akin to brute and half akin to man. A kind of selfish intelligence characterizes their thinking. They lack a sense of proportion and relation. Before the ant a man looms as large as a mountain before us. An insect does not see things as they are but as they seem to it. Growth in intelligence necessitates a truer appreciation of proportions and relations. The pigmy also sees little but himself, but years and experience leave behind them wisdom. The civilized races have all risen from barbarism and savagery - that is, from a state of imperfect thinking as well as of imperfect loving and choosing. Experience and culture bring larger knowledge and a more equable balance of the faculties. No man should be measured by his achievement in any one field of endeavor. He may paint like Titian and be as voluptuous; he may write tragedies like Shakespeare and have no logic; he may be a gatherer of facts like Darwin and have no power of philosophic analysis. The intellect grows steadily toward perfection of vision and logical strength, and also and quite as significantly, toward harmony in the development of all the powers of thought.

The contrast between the selfish cunning of an African pigmy and the large and noble minds which are steadily multiplying, is a prophecy of the man who will dwell on this earth when the vision is clear and the power of rational judgment is perfected.

The prophecy of the soul is not less evident in the emotional nature. At first the soul is either so imperfect, or so limited by the body, that it seems to be nothing but a creature of emotions. It loves, but its affections are selfish and egotistic. What may be called the epochs in its growth are finely treated by Coleridge in "The Ancient Mariner" and by Tennyson in "In Memoriam." The Ancient Mariner felt only selfish affection. He had no love for "being as being." He killed the albatross with as little heed as he disregarded his fellow-men;

but the ministries of his misery were multiplied until, at length, he was able to see something beautiful even in the writhing green sea-serpents that followed the ship of death on which he sailed. That was the first sign of the larger interest which had long been growing within him, and which was to continue to grow until he could say,

"He prayeth best who loveth best
All things both great and small."

"In Memoriam" is the record of the expansion of a soul through its increase in love. At the beginning of his grief the poet sings, dolefully and hopelessly, through his tears,

"He is not here; but far away
The noise of life begins again,
And ghastly thro' the drizzling rain
On the bald street breaks the blank day."

But the soul is growing secretly and surely as wheat grows in winter. The Christmas bells ring out their music and at first are almost hated, but they break through the shell of sorrow and let in a faint echo of the world's great suffering and the world's great joy. Thus human sympathy is enlarged just a bit. In successive years the music of the Christmas bells is heard more distinctly, the sorrow of the world becomes more audible, sympathy reaches farther. At last the poem which began with a *miserere* ends with a marriage, and he who could at first write that dreary line,

"On the bald street breaks the blank day"

testifies to the beneficence of the path in which he had been led in this wise and beautiful stanza,

"Regret is dead, but love is more
Than in the summers that have flown,
For I myself with these have grown
To something greater than before."

From dwelling in a prison with grief as a jailer he has caught a vision of the,

> "One far off divine event
> To which the whole creation moves."

This expansion of the soul is not difficult to follow. Traces of it may be seen in the enlarged sympathy, the growing brotherhood, and in the rapidly increasing conviction that even nationalities are only temporary expedients for bringing the day when love shall be the universal law. The charities and philanthropies which are blossoming in every city and country district, the consciousness of responsibility for the poor and weak, the angel songs which are heard in the midst of battle, and the gradual disappearance of war, are all vague but true prophecies of what the soul will be when love is perfected. The knowledge of past progress is an inspiration, and the imagination of what will be a glorious hope.

A single clause in the Apocalypse has long seemed to me as fine a statement of the condition which will prevail, when this prophecy is a reality, as could be phrased, - "The Lamb is the light thereof." Light is the medium in which objects are visible, and the Lamb is the symbol of sacrificial love. The great dreamer, in his vision, beheld a time when spirits would see in sacrificial love as now we see physical objects in the medium of light. To those who have studied the expansion of individual souls, and who then have contrasted the selfishness of earlier social conditions with the love of men as it is revealed in the laws, institutions, ministries of to-day, this dream of the Apostle rises in the distance as a new continent to a voyager over the wide and desolate ocean.

Equally prophetic is the advance which has been made from the passion of savage barbarism, or infantile wilfulness, to the moral reason of the present day as seen in the highest types of humanity in civilized lands. Wilfulness characterizes the childish nature and passion the savage nature. But with the growth of the soul choices are differentiated from impulses, and more and more regularly are inspired by intelligence and unselfish affection. This progress toward intelligent and unselfish choice distinguishes the movement toward civilization. Here, again, the advance made by the individual soul and by the race are equally prophetic. With the years the choices become more rational and loving. Time mellows all men somewhat, and forces a little wisdom into the hardest heads. Even slight growth prophesies that which shall be swifter when conditions are more favorable.

The soul is a prediction of clearer vision, truer thought, more unselfish love and wiser choices. It is a prophecy of the perfect man.

History is also prophetic of larger souls. The stream of human history, after it has been followed backward a few thousand years, leads into the region of legend and myth - that is, to a time when history could not be written because there was no writing, and when all truth was conveyed in symbolical forms. That means toward a time of narrow experience, and of knowledge far more limited than the present. Memory, in those days, was enormously and abnormally capacious and retentive, but there was no appreciation of humanity. Few lessons from the experiences of others were possible, because the mind was filled with merely tribal legends. What was called early civilization was only relatively splendid. There was unsurpassed poetry but no science, ample brawn but diminutive brain, much passion but little love. Out of the darkness of the past the stream of history, very narrow and shallow at first, has emerged and steadily expanded and deepened. Men are now equally intense but far clearer in vision, nobler in purpose, and purer in character. Their laws year by year have become more humane, their sympathies less contracted, their institutions more civilized. Nature's secret drawers have been unlocked. We are sometimes told that science has added much to the store of man's knowledge but nothing to the strength of his mind or the nobility of his character. That is a serious mistake. With the enlarged visions of the universe, with clearer conceptions of our cosmic relations, with the national neighborliness which is now a necessity, the capacity and the quality of the soul must change. Nay, it has already changed, for we inhabit the same lands over which savages formerly roamed, and we find in the earth and air what they never found; and when we look up into the great wide sky and say, "The Heavens declare the glory of God," we are not thinking of a tribal Deity, or a partial, and more or less passionate, monarch enthroned in the midst of his splendors, but of the King Eternal, immortal, invisible. Knowledge tends to enlarge the mind by which it is acquired. All faculties are strengthened by use.

History has moved along a bloody pathway, or, to revert to the figure of a stream, is indeed a river of "tears and blood." The horrors of the process by which the race has been lifted can hardly be exaggerated. I do not forget them while I put stronger emphasis on the fact that the outcome of all the struggle of individuals, the conflict of classes, and the wars of nations has been a nobler and purer quality of soul, - not less heroic but more sacrificial, not less strong but far more virtuous.

The growth of the individual soul is mirrored in the progress of the race. When we have learned to read aright the history of the world, we are informed as to the interior forces which have made civilization. Events are expressions of thoughts; institutions are manifestations of soul. If there has been progress in institutions there must have been an equal progress in the souls which are the real forces by which progress is always won. As history has been the evolution of humanity toward finer forms, so it is the assurance that the forces which have been at work in the past will not cease, but steadily continue until "the pile is complete." The perfect society will be composed of perfected individuals. History as prophecy is harmonious with soul as prophecy.

The future state of the soul has been the subject of rare fascination for the world's great thinkers. Nearly all religions have a forward look. "The Golden Age" lies far in the distance, but it has commanded the faith of all the seers. It has sometimes been a dream concerning individuals, and again a vision of the perfected society, but in reality the two are one, for the social organism is but a congeries of individuals. Bacon dreamed of New Atlantis, Sir Thomas More saw the fair walls of Utopia rising in the future, Plato defined the boundaries of the ideal Republic, Augustine wrote of the glories of the *Civitate Dei*, and Tennyson with matchless music has sung of the crowning race: -

"Ring out old shapes of foul disease;
Ring out the narrowing lust of gold;
Ring out the thousand wars of old,
Ring in the thousand years of peace.

Ring in the valiant man and free,
The larger heart, the kindlier hand;
Ring out the darkness of the land,
Ring in the Christ that is to be."

The common characteristic of these social ideals is their dependence on the culture of individuals. With the incoming of "the valiant man and free," the man of "larger heart and kindlier hand," there is a reasonable hope that the darkness of the land will disappear.

With that deep look into the inmost secrets of human experience which sounds strangely autobiographical, Browning wrote in "Rabbi Ben Ezra,"

"Praise be thine!
I see the whole design,
I, who saw power, see love now perfect too;
Perfect I call thy plan;
Thanks that I was a man!
Maker, remake, complete, - I trust what Thou shalt do!"

"Therefore I summon age
To grant youth's heritage,

Life's struggle having so far reached its term;
Thence shall I pass, approved
A man, for aye removed
From the developed brute; a god though in the germ."

Those last lines condense Browning's creed concerning man. He is "for aye removed from the developed brute," and is "a god in the germ." Browning holds that while in the future there will surely be expansion of soul, evolution as a physical process is at an end. Henceforward there will be no passing from one species to another. Species have to do with physical organisms, not with spirits. Soul in man is but God "in the germ."

Emerson and Matthew Arnold have written much about education. The one foretells a day when the soul, after mounting and meliorating, finds that even the hells are turned into benefit; and the other makes his own the thought of Bishop Wilson that culture is a study of perfection, and that the soul must ever seek increased life, increased light, and increased power.

Education is the word of the hour and of the century. It is believed to be the panacea for all ills, individual and social. But, precisely, what does this passion for education signify if not that, either intelligently or otherwise, all believe in the perfectibility of the soul, and that it will have all the time that it needs for the process. The absorbing devotion to intellectual training suggests the inquiry as to whether many who affirm that they are agnostic concerning immortality are not in reality earnest in their faith; for why should they seek the culture of that which fades, as the flowers fade; when it approaches life's winter? But, whether faith in continuance of being is firm or frail, few doubt the perfectibility of spirit, because, beyond almost all things, they are seeking its perfection. Literature, which is but the thoughts of the great souls of successive periods recorded, prophesies a day when all that hinders or taints shall be done away, and when the divine in the germ shall have grown to large and fair proportions. If there were no

Amory H. Bradford

other light the outlook would still be inspiring. It is well sometimes to ask ourselves what we were made to be - not these bodies which are clearly decaying - but these spirits which seem to grow younger with the passage of time. I have sometimes thought that the very idea of second childhood is itself a prophecy of the soul's eternal youth. Certain it is that we are the masters of the years. The oldest persons that we know are usually the youngest in their sympathies and ideals. Sorrow and opposition should not destroy, but only strengthen the spiritual powers. Intelligence grows from more to more. The sure reward of love is the capacity and opportunity for larger love. Virtuous choices gradually become the law of liberty. These facts are index fingers pointing toward large and loving, strenuous and sympathetic manhood. And toward such human types, as a matter of fact, the race has been moving. The expectation of the seers and prophets, also, has been of a golden age in which all souls will have had time, and opportunity, of reaching the far-off but splendid goal. Believing, as we do, that death is never a finality, but that it is only an incident in progress; that instead of being an end it is only freedom from limitation, we find ourselves often vaguely, but ever eagerly, asking, To what are all these souls tending? Toward a state glorious beyond language to utter we deeply feel. But has no clearer voice spoken? At last we have reached the end of our inquiry. If any other voices speak they must sound from above. We stand by the unseen like children by the ocean's shore. They know that beyond the storms and waves lie fair and wealthy lands, but the waters separate and their eyes are weak. So we stand before the future, and ask, Toward what goal are all this education, experience and discipline tending? Are they perfecting souls which at last are to be laid away with the bodies which were fortunate enough to win an earlier death? It would be impiety to believe that. Then indeed should we be put to "permanent intellectual confusion." If all the voices of the soul are mockeries, then life is worse than a mistake - it is a crime.

The solution of the mystery is now before us. The man that is to be has walked this earth, and wrought with human hands, and lived and labored and loved, and passed into the silent land. Is Jesus the unique revelation of the divine? There may be many to question that, but there are few, indeed, who doubt that He embodied all of the perfect humanity which could be expressed within the limitations of the body. He represented Himself as essential truth and very life. He condensed duty into such love as He manifested toward men. He embodied the heroism of meekness, the courage of self-sacrifice, the vision of goodness. He was an example of all that is strong, serene, sacrificial, in the midst of the lowest and most unresponsive conditions. So much we see, and the rest we dimly, but surely, feel.

It was reserved for Paul, in a moment of inspiration, to put into a single phrase a description of the goal of the human spirit, as something which may be forever approached but never reached, in these words, "Till we all attain unto the measure of the stature of the fullness of Christ." The fullness of Christ! That is the soul's final destiny. It was the far call of that goal which it faintly heard at its first awakening and which has never entirely ceased to sound in his ears. Who shall explore the contents of that great phrase? It is a subject for meditation, for prayer, but never for discussion. He who approaches it in a controversial spirit never understands it. What are the qualities of the character of Christ? Some of them lie on the surface of the story. He never doubted God, or, if so, but for a single moment; He was unselfish; He lived to love and to express love; He had some mysterious preternatural power over nature - such, perhaps, as science is approaching in later times; kindness, sympathy, helpfulness, purity, shone from His words and actions. He declared that the privilege of dying to save those who despised Him was a joy. He lived in the limitations of the human condition and, therefore, on the earth only hints of "His fullness" are discernible. The full revelation is to be the endless study of those who are able to see and to appreciate things as they are. But we may ask ourselves whither these lines tend. When the intelligence, the love, the compassion, the mercy, the purity, the moral power and spiritual grandeur which only in dim outline are revealed in the Christ, have perfect manifestations, what will the vision be? The very thought transcends the farthest flights of the poet's imagination and the most daring speculations of philosophers. In "the fullness of Christ" is the soul's true goal. For that all men, and not the elect few, were created. That is the revelation of the divine plan for humanity. Toward that evolution has been slowly, and often painfully, pressing from those dim aeons when the earth was without form and void. When man appeared as the flower of all the cosmic process he started at once toward this goal. And with great modesty, and simply because I believe in God and that His love cannot be defeated, I dare to hope that, sometime and somehow, after all the pains of retribution and moral discipline have done their inevitable work, after all the fires of Gehenna have consumed the desire to sin, after Hades and Purgatory have been passed, the souls which, for a time, have dwelt in these mortal bodies, purified and without spot or wrinkle or any such thing, will be given the beatific vision and permitted to realize the height and depth, the length and breadth of "the fullness of Christ."

"That one Face, far from vanish, rather grows,
Or decomposes but to recompose,
Become my universe that feels and knows."

Choose from Thousands of 1stWorldLibrary Classics By

Ada Leverson	Charles Ives	Evelyn Everett-green
Adolphus William Ward	Charles Kingsley	Everard Cotes
Aesop	Charles Klein	F. H. Cheley
Agatha Christie	Charles Lathrop Pack	F. J. Cross
Alexander Aaronsohn	Charles Whibley	Federick Austin Ogg
Alexander Kielland	Charles Willing Beale	Ferdinand Ossendowski
Alexandre Dumas	Charlotte M. Braeme	Francis Bacon
Alfred Gatty	Charlotte M. Yonge	Francis Darwin
Alfred Ollivant	Charlotte Perkins Stetson	Frances Hodgson Burnett
Alice Duer Miller	Clair W. Hayes	Frances Parkinson Keyes
Alice Turner Curtis	Clarence Day Jr.	Frank Gee Patchin
Alice Dunbar	Clarence E. Mulford	Frank Harris
Ambrose Bierce	Clemence Housman	Frank Jewett Mather
Amelia E. Barr	Confucius	Frank L. Packard
Andrew Lang	Cornelis DeWitt Wilcox	Frank V. Webster
Andrew McFarland Davis	Cyril Burleigh	Frederic Stewart Isham
Andy Adams	D. H. Lawrence	Frederick Trevor Hill
Anna Sewell	Daniel Defoe	Frederick Winslow Taylor
Annie Besant	David Garnett	Friedrich Kerst
Annie Hamilton Donnell	Don Carlos Janes	Friedrich Nietzsche
Annie Payson Call	Donald Keyhoe	Fyodor Dostoyevsky
Annonaymous	Dorothy Kilner	G.A. Henty
Anton Chekhov	Dougan Clark	G.K. Chesterton
Arnold Bennett	Douglas Fairbanks	Gabrielle E. Jackson
Arthur Conan Doyle	E. Nesbit	Garrett P. Serviss
Arthur M. Winfield	E.P.Roe	Gaston Leroux
Arthur Ransome	E. Phillips Oppenheim	George Ade
Atticus	Edgar Rice Burroughs	Geroge Bernard Shaw
B.H. Baden-Powell	Edith Van Dyne	George Durston
B. M. Bower	Edith Wharton	George Ebers
Baroness Emmuska Orczy	Edward J. O'Biren	George Eliot
Baroness Orczy	Edward S. Ellis	George MacDonald
Basil King	Edwin L. Arnold	George Meredith
Bayard Taylor	Eleanor Atkins	George Orwell
Ben Macomber	Eliot Gregory	George Tucker
Bertha Muzzy Bower	Elizabeth Gaskell	George W. Cable
Bjornstjerne Bjornson	Elizabeth McCracken	George Wharton James
Booth Tarkington	Elizabeth Von Arnim	Gertrude Atherton
Boyd Cable	Ellem Key	Grace E. King
Bram Stoker	Emerson Hough	Grace Gallatin
C. Collodi	Emily Dickinson	Grant Allen
C. E. Orr	Enid Bagnold	Guillermo A. Sherwell
C. M. Ingleby	Enilor Macartney Lane	Gulielma Zollinger
Carolyn Wells	Erasmus W. Jones	Gustav Flaubert
Catherine Parr Traill	Ernie Howard Pie	H. A. Cody
Charles A. Eastman	Ethel Turner	H. B. Irving
Charles Dickens	Ethel Watts Mumford	H.C. Bailey
Charles Dudley Warner	Eugenie Foa	H. G. Wells
Charles Farrar Browne	Eugene Wood	H. H. Munro

H. Irving Hancock	James DeMille	Louisa May Alcott
H. Rider Haggard	James Joyce	Lucy Fitch Perkins
H. W. C. Davis	James Lane Allen	Lucy Maud Montgomery
Hamilton Wright Mabie	James Lane Allen	Lydia Miller Middleton
Hans Christian Andersen	James Oliver Curwood	Lyndon Orr
Harold Avery	James Oppenheim	M. Corvus
Harold McGrath	James Otis	M. H. Adams
Harriet Beecher Stowe	James R. Driscoll	Margaret E. Sangster
Harry Houidini	Jane Austen	Margaret Vandercook
Helent Hunt Jackson	Jens Peter Jacobsen	Margret Penrose
Helen Nicolay	Jerome K. Jerome	Maria Edgeworth
Hendrik Conscience	John Burroughs	Maria Thompson Daviess
Hendy David Thoreau	John Cournos	Mariano Azuela
Henri Barbusse	John F. Kennedy	Marion Polk Angellotti
Henrik Ibsen	John Gay	Mark Overton
Henry Adams	John Glasworthy	Mark Twain
Henry Ford	John Habberton	Mary Austin
Henry Frost	John Joy Bell	Mary Catherine Crowley
Henry James	John Kendrick Bangs	Mary Cole
Henry Jones Ford	John Milton	Mary Hastings Bradley
Henry Seton Merriman	John Philip Sousa	Mary Roberts Rinehart
Henry W Longfellow	Jonas Lauritz Idemil Lie	Mary Rowlandson
Herbert A. Giles	Jonathan Swift	M. Wollstonecraft Shelley
Herbert N. Casson	Joseph A. Altsheler	Maud Lindsay
Herman Hesse	Joseph Carey	Max Beerbohm
Homer	Joseph Conrad	Myra Kelly
Honore De Balzac	Joseph E. Badger Jr	Nathaniel Hawthrone
Horace Walpole	Joseph Hergesheimer	Nicolo Machiavelli
Horatio Alger Jr.	Joseph Jacobs	O. F. Walton
Howard Pyle	Julian Hawthrone	Oscar Wilde
Howard R. Garis	Julies Vernes	Owen Johnson
Hugh Lofting	Justin Huntly McCarthy	P.G. Wodehouse
Hugh Walpole	Kakuzo Okakura	Paul and Mabel Thorne
Humphry Ward	Kenneth Grahame	Paul G. Tomlinson
Ian Maclaren	Kenneth McGaffey	Paul Severing
Inez Haynes Gillmore	Kate Langley Bosher	Percy Brebner
Irving Bacheller	Kate Langley Bosher	Peter B. Kyne
Israel Abrahams	Katherine Cecil Thurston	Plato
Ivan Turgenev	Katherine Stokes	R. Derby Holmes
J.G.Austin	L. A. Abbot	R. L. Stevenson
J. Henri Fabre	L. T. Meade	R. S. Ball
J. M. Barrie	L. Frank Baum	Rabindranath Tagore
J. Macdonald Oxley	Latta Griswold	Rahul Alvares
J. S. Fletcher	Laura Lee Hope	Ralph Henry Barbour
J. S. Knowles	Laurence Housman	Ralph Waldo Emmerson
J. Storer Clouston	Leo Tolstoy	Rene Descartes
Jack London	Leonid Andreyev	Rex Beach
Jacob Abbott	Lewis Carroll	Rex E. Beach
James Allen	Lilian Bell	Richard Harding Davis
James Andrews	Lloyd Osbourne	Richard Jefferies
James Baldwin	Louis Tracy	Richard Le Gallienne

Robert Barr
Robert Frost
Robert Gordon Anderson
Robert L. Drake
Robert Lansing
Robert Lynd
Robert Michael Ballantyne
Robert W. Chambers
Rosa Nouchette Carey
Rudyard Kipling
Samuel B. Allison
Samuel Hopkins Adams
Sarah Bernhardt
Selma Lagerlof
Sherwood Anderson
Sigmund Freud
Standish O'Grady
Stanley Weyman
Stella Benson
Stephen Crane
Stewart Edward White
Stijn Streuvels
Swami Abhedananda

Swami Parmananda
T. S. Ackland
T. S. Arthur
The Princess Der Ling
Thomas A. Janvier
Thomas A Kempis
Thomas Anderton
Thomas Bailey Aldrich
Thomas Bulfinch
Thomas De Quincey
Thomas H. Huxley
Thomas Hardy
Thomas More
Thornton W. Burgess
U. S. Grant
Valentine Williams
Various Authors
Victor Appleton
Virginia Woolf
Walter Camp
Walter Scott
Washington Irving
Wilbur Lawton

Wilkie Collins
Willa Cather
Willard F. Baker
William Dean Howells
William le Queux
W. Makepeace Thackeray
William W. Walter
Winston Churchill
Yei Theodora Ozaki
Yogi Ramacharaka
Young E. Allison
Zane Grey